CW00725111

C. F. Roe was brou.... ... .
from Aberdeen University Medical School with a
gold medal in surgery. He has practised and taught
surgery in the US, travelled the world as a ship's
surgeon and worked in Afghanistan before becoming
a full-time writer. C. F. Roe now lives in Albuquerque,
New Mexico.

PART ONE

A Death in the Family

C. F. Roe

HEADLINE

First published in 1993
by HEADLINE BOOK PUBLISHING PLC

First published in paperback in 1993
by HEADLINE BOOK PUBLISHING PLC

10 9 8 7 6 5 4 3 2 1

ISBN 0 7472 4089 2

Printed and bound in Great Britain by
HarperCollins Manufacturing, Glasgow

HEADLINE BOOK PUBLISHING PLC
Headline House
79 Great Titchfield Street
London W1P 7FN

Chapter One

For the third day in succession, a windless, silent snow had fallen over central Scotland, and it was still coming down when Rory McDermott climbed out of bed. The old springs creaked, and Bella, his common-law wife, made a groaning noise and turned over, her right arm flopping over his still-warm pillow. It was only two-thirty in the morning, but Rory didn't need an alarm clock. He had never used one, not since the first time his father had quietly shaken him awake at this hour, some fifteen years before. But there was something different about tonight; a strange compulsion that he only partly understood.

Rory knew it would be cold out; by the time he got home again he'd be chilled to the bone. He felt for his clothes; as usual, they were ready on the chair by the bed. Having thrown off his pyjama top, he shivered and pulled on a long-sleeved woollen semmit next to his skin, then two thin sweaters over that, the red one on the inside. He pulled the sleeves down to keep them loose around his oxters, then fumbled into a big, loose-fitting cable-stitch sweater. Rory put on two pairs of thick once-white socks, a pair of old dark twill pants over his pyjama bottoms, and then he padded quietly out of the room.

Bella had set out a thick corned-beef-and-cheese

sandwich for him next to a big thermos on the draining
board. Rory heated the milky tea in a pan, added four
spoonfuls of sugar, and poured the liquid into the
thermos, up to the top, then he put his meal into his
bag. He would certainly need the heat and sustenance by
the time he'd finished. His boots, dark parka and black
woollen bonnet were by the back door, and the rest of
his gear was already in his car.

Outside, he walked into a thick, padded, snowy
silence. Rory could see the dim orange lights of Perth
reflected in the low clouds over the city to his right. The
snow was still coming down, but less strongly now, and
Rory felt sure it would stop soon. The car was parked at
the side of the house. Snow covered the windscreen, and
Rory brushed it off with his bare hands, then clumped
around to clear the rear window. The ancient black
Morris was scratched and battered, but it started on the
first turn of the key, and after a few moments, ran
quietly and smoothly. Rory always made sure that the
important parts of his car, like the rest of his
equipment, were kept in perfect repair.

There was no traffic, and ten minutes later, the car
was rolling quietly along the deserted Dunkeld Road
towards the Almond Bridge. A couple of miles further
along, without having passed a single vehicle, Rory
turned right into a narrow, unpaved road. The snow
had stopped, and the almost-full moon appeared
intermittently from behind the rapidly moving clouds.
He switched off the car's headlights. Even after all the
times he had been here, an excitement rose in him, a
feeling of wariness and caution, almost dread, as he
guided the car around the well-remembered potholes
hidden beneath the smooth snow.

Having parked the car, out of sight under an arch of
the railway bridge, Rory took his equipment out of the
boot and pulled on his waders. The River Tay was some
fifty yards beyond the bridge, and it took him several
minutes to reach the bank. It wasn't easy to keep his

balance because he was carrying his gear, and he slithered on the icy bank and almost fell a couple of times before clambering down to the water's edge.

Rory was an old-fashioned poacher who took pride in his old-fashioned methods. A waterproof lantern, a box of tried and true lures, a good rod and a short wooden club to stun the fish were his stock in trade, and he despised the *parvenu* poachers who gave the occupation a bad name with their diving equipment, spearguns and explosives. Rory was drawn to a pool close to the opposite side of the river, shaded by high trees near the bank, half a mile downstream from the edge of the Dalgleish estate, a place he gave a wide berth to nowadays. The pool was in an unlikely spot at the end of a sandbar, and had served him well over the years; the salmon knew the waters and he'd often find one or two big ones resting, still but watchful, in its cool peaty depth. A light, chilling wind started to blow down the river from the North, and Rory felt the cold beginning to invade his feet and legs as he waded out into the knee-high water, every sense alert, although he felt pretty sure that tonight the bailiffs would be staying comfortably in their beds.

After half-an-hour's methodical fishing, Rory was pretty sure there was nothing in the pool, and was thinking about trying further down the river when his lure snagged close to the bank. Unwilling to lose the lure, he manoeuvred himself cautiously around the pool to get closer to the bank. Under the trees it was even darker than on the river, and he followed his line with his hand where it went under the water. It seemed to be snagged in the roots a foot or so under the surface, and feeling blindly with his right hand, holding on to the extinguished lantern and the rod with his left, he first encountered what seemed like thin, wavy grass then something smooth and slimy that moved slightly when he touched it. For a moment he felt around, trying to find the metal lure, then he realized what it was attached to. Choking on a yell of sheer terror, Rory fell backwards into the water with a splash, then scrambled up and floundered back towards the other side of the river, unheedful, for the first time in his life, of the splashing and disturbance he was making. Soaked and frozen, and half-frightened out of his life, he stumbled up the steep bank, his numb feet squelching in the waterlogged waders. When he got back to the car, panting and out of breath, he leaned against the bonnet and vomited painfully. Then, still shaking, he put his gear in the boot and started the drive back to the main road.

It was still dark when he got back home. Bella heard him and sat up in bed with a start. She knew that something was wrong by the way he came in the house.

'Bailiffs?' she asked, when he came into the room, letting a flurry of cold air in with him. She pulled the sheet up around her chest.

Rory told her what he had found.

'You'd better call the police,' said Bella, her eyes wide. 'You don't need to tell them who you are.'

'They would trace the call,' replied Rory heavily. He sat down in the chair and stretched out his legs. 'Here, help me get these waders off.'

Five minutes later, Bella, dressed and muffled up in her coat and gloves, went down to the phone box at the end of the lane. By some miracle it was working, and she dialled 999 and hurriedly told the officer who answered where he should look for the body. She didn't answer his questions and hung up quickly, breathing hard.

It was still pitch dark, and the snow was falling again. Bella tightened the scarf around her neck and started to walk home.

Chapter Two

When the phone rang, Jean Montrose's first thought, almost before she was awake enough to realize that it was ringing, was the noise must not wake Steven. He grunted and turned when she reached over and picked up the receiver.

'Jean? I hate to call you so early in the morning . . .' Inspector Douglas Niven's voice was apologetic.

She looked at the luminous dial of the clock on the bedside table. 'It's all right, Doug. I was getting up in a few minutes anyway. What's the matter?'

'You know the Dalgleish girl, Moira, who's been missing for over a week now?'

Jean sat up bed, alert, steeling herself for bad news. 'Yes, Douglas. Moira's a patient of mine.'

'Well, I think we found her just a wee while ago. In the Tay. From the looks of her, she'd been there for some time.'

'Oh, my God . . .' Jean had an instant vision of Moira Dalgleish walking down South Street in Perth; confident, straight-backed and beautiful in a white blouse, a kilt swinging around her bare, tanned legs, blond hair streaming behind her and every man in the area watching her, boldly or out of the corner of his eye.

'Her poor little baby,' she murmured, mostly to herself. 'Is Malcolm Anderson up there with you?' Jean was referring to the local police surgeon and pathologist.

'No. He's off in Glasgow for some meeting.'

Jean sighed. 'OK, I suppose you want me to come out. Where are you?'

'I'm at the station, just leaving. I sent Jamieson out wi' a couple of men when the call came in, and he's just reported back. I'll see you in a wee while.'

Doug Niven picked Jean up twenty minutes later. Jean didn't care for driving with Doug very much, and she ostentatiously strapped herself in tight, hoping he would take the hint.

But Doug had his mind on other things. 'I called the family,' he said. 'One of them's going to come down to identify the body.'

'Why do you think it's Moira, Douglas?' said Jean, still hoping that it might be someone else. It seemed impossible that a woman as full of life as the splendid Moira Dalgleish could be dead.

'We had a description when she went missing. She was wearing a gold ring with the Dalgleish seal on it, and a bracelet with those blue stones on it, I forget what they're called.'

'Turquoises?' suggested Jean, closing her eyes for a moment as the car hit a patch of ice and slid broadside around a corner and on to the Isla Road. Douglas twisted the wheel, and the vehicle slithered then straightened and sped along the road. A car nosed out of Kincarrathie Crescent in front of him and Doug missed it by inches.

'Douglas!' Jean tried to think of something that would slow him down. 'Have you forgotten you're soon to be a father? Do you want the poor bairn to grow up without a dad?'

That did it, although Douglas was truly convinced that he was driving rather sedately. He slowed down and the rest of the journey was completed at a more reasonable speed. Half a mile before the main entrance to the Dalgleish estate, Douglas slowed and turned left into the service road. There were already several vehicle tracks in the snow. The road was very bumpy and Doug's car slid a few times, but after a couple of hundred yards they could faintly see trees and the river beyond them. The road widened into an open space, large enough for a car to turn in, and Douglas parked the car next to a black police van. Further downstream, through the large bare trees that lined the river bank, they could see the glow of the police emergency team's portable floodlights, still on although the dawn was already spreading over the hills, casting an unwilling grey light over the scene. To Jean, the river looked cold, evil and unforgiving, quite unlike its usual sparkling appearance, as if its normal joyfulness had been unmasked to reveal its underlying sinister self.

Twenty yards downstream and a few yards from the bank, a police diver in a black wet-suit was up to his hips in the water. As Doug and Jean watched, his feet slipped and he disappeared with a splash. A moment later his head reappeared. He shook his head and spat water out of his mouth.

'There's a bloody deep pool down here,' he shouted, sounding a little embarrassed.

Douglas ignored him. 'Where was she?' he asked Jamieson, who was coming out of the shallow water near the bank, looking pale and sick.

'In those roots down there, sir,' he said, pointing towards the riverbank. He studiously ignored Jean, whom he perceived as an ancient enemy ever since the time she'd almost killed him during the Lumsden baby investigation. Jamieson's sleeves and uniform trousers were soaked, and Jean guessed that getting Moira out of the water must have been a messy business; she had been reported missing eight days before, and although the weather had been cold, if she'd been in the water that long, her body would already be falling apart. The stretcher and its burden lay unattended on the ground just a few feet away from the bank, covered with a white sheet.

Jean gritted her teeth and went over to it. Strands of long blonde hair hung over the edge of the stretcher. She pulled back the sheet. Jean was sure that it was Moira, although the woman was next to unrecognizable. Her face was puffy and pale, the skin was grey-white and bloated with absorbed water, and the eyes were flat and collapsed, making her face, so recently full of sparkle and liveliness, look grotesque and bloated. Several small black objects stuck to her skin, on her cheeks and nose. Jean pushed one of the objects with her nail, then realized it was a small mollusc, firmly attached.

'I had a hold of her arm, and I was trying to pull her out,' Jamieson was saying to Doug, a few feet away. His face showed his revulsion. 'Then her skin started to slide off the flesh. I'm sorry . . .'

Jean couldn't repress a shudder. But, somehow, hearing what Jamieson said, together with seeing the body, had blurred her vivid and painful memory of Moira in life.

'How long do you think she was in the water?' asked Doug, coming over to the stretcher.

'I'm not a pathologist, you know,' said Jean, a little more sharply than she intended. 'But I would guess maybe a week. The water temperature would be a couple of degrees above freezing, and the rate of putrefaction in running water is usually about half of what it is in the open air, if I remember rightly. Do any of your people have a thermometer?'

'It's one point five Celsius,' said the diver, who was just then clambering up on the bank. He was young, tall, with a sandy moustache. His face and hands were bright red and he was shivering in spite of his wet suit. He was holding a wriggling, foot-long eel in his hand. 'The place is alive with these,' he said, and threw the creature back into the water.

'Thanks, Terry,' said Doug. He turned to the two

men leaning against the black police van. 'OK, you two, you can put her in the back now.' He scowled at them. 'Come on, get moving.'

They all turned when they heard the faint sound of a car on the main road. The vehicle slowed, and they saw the headlights swing round like beacons. As the car got closer, there was just enough light for Doug to make out that it was a Jaguar, making heavy weather of the huge bumps and potholes in the road, and lurching like a drunken duchess down the narrow road towards them. They watched as the car pulled up next to the police van, on the other side of Doug's car, and a tall man in his mid forties climbed out. He was wearing a tweed cap and a heavy woollen overcoat. Jean noticed that he had lightweight shoes quite unsuited to the deep snow.

It was Alastair Dalgleish, MP, Moira's uncle. He came towards them with a grim expression, obviously prepared for bad news.

'Moira's father is . . . unable to come,' he said. 'Are you sure it's her?' Alastair's voice was steady, but Jean could see his eyes, flickering from Doug to her, and she felt a surge of compassion for him, for all those who had loved his niece.

'We think the person we found drowned is Moira Dalgleish, sir,' replied Douglas, as usual, dry-mouthed and tongue-tied in the presence of gentry. He indicated the back of the van, where the two policemen were struggling to lift the stretcher.

'Can I see her?' asked Alastair quietly.

Douglas glanced at Jean, but she made no sign. It was none of her business.

'I suppose that would be permissible, sir,' he said reluctantly, 'But I have to warn you that she's not a pretty sight at this point in time, sir.'

Dalgleish turned and went to the van. One of the men helped him up, and supplemented the faint interior light with a big portable lantern while he pulled back the sheet. Dalgleish stared at the white face for a long moment, then turned away. He tripped and almost fell getting out of the van.

'I confirm that that is my niece, Moira Dalgleish.' He said her name with a peculiar inflection of finality, then turned to walk slowly back towards his car.

'We'll need to come later to talk to you and your family, sir,' Doug called after him. Without looking around, Alastair lifted a hand to acknowledge that he had heard, then climbed back into his car. The door clunked, and as the vehicle turned before going back up the road, they caught a glimpse of Alastair's wife Patricia, her blonde hair and pale face enclosed in a dark tartan shawl. She was sitting in the back of the car, looking straight ahead of her. Patricia Dalgleish didn't look as if she needed sympathy or support from anyone.

'Do you know if she was depressed?' asked Doug, as they drove back towards Perth.

'Moira? Not that I know of,' replied Jean carefully. 'In fact, she seemed full of life and happy with her baby last time I saw her. She brought him in to the surgery for his six-month check-up only a couple of weeks ago.'

'What about her husband? I heard something about him . . .'

Jean closed her eyes. They were coming up to the red light where the Isla Road joined the Dundee Road at Bridgend, and it didn't seem possible that Douglas could stop in time. He did, although all the wheels of his car were locked when it came to rest, and the vehicle finished up almost at right angles to the road.

'I'm sure I don't know any more than you, Douglas,' she replied, keeping her voice level and loosening her grip on the dashboard. 'I never met him.'

'Somebody told me he'd died,' said Douglas. 'Actually before the baby was born. Sad, that.' He turned into Alford Street, then left, up the curving hill towards Jean's house on Argyll Crescent.

'Well, Douglas, the way you drive, the same could happen to you.'

Doug looked over at Jean in surprise, 'They way I drive? Do you know I completed the advanced police driver's course in Glasgow last year?'

'Oh yes?' A tiny smile lurked around Jean's eyes. 'What did they teach you?'

'How to get out of bad situations, mostly,' replied Douglas. 'For instance, when you're following dangerous criminals and want to get them off the road,' Douglas's hands tightened on the steering wheel as he remembered the huge police car-park with the oily surface on which cars seemed to slide for ever, 'you give them a nudge in the back quarter, from the side, you know, and that destabilizes them immediately and they go out of control . . .'

'I'll be sure to remember that, Douglas, thank you,' murmured Jean. 'Maybe I'll try it next time I go shopping and somebody cuts me off.'

'I wouldn't do that if I were you,' said Douglas seriously. 'You'd need special training . . . Anyway, here we are,' he went on, pulling up outside Jean's house. 'All ship-shape and Bristol fashion.'

'He died in Hong Kong,' said Jean. 'A very nice young man, from all accounts.'

Doug stared at her for a second. 'Oh, Moira's husband. I wonder who's going to take care of the baby.'

Moira's mother, I suppose,' replied Jean. She turned towards Douglas, her hand on the door handle. 'Do you think that could have been a suicide back there, Douglas?'

'We'll know soon enough after Malcolm Anderson's been at her,' he replied. 'I didn't see any signs of injury, did you?'

'Hard to tell, in the condition she was in.' Jean looked puzzled for a second as if something had crossed her mind. 'But if she did commit suicide, something terrible must have happened in her life within the last two weeks. When I saw her she was looking on top of the world.'

'Did you think that was a bit strange?' asked Doug. 'Being on top of the world? With her being a young widow with a bairn to take care of and no husband to look after her?'

'Things are a bit different nowadays,' said Jean. 'Women don't expect to be taken care of as much as they used to. Most of us work, and in a pinch we can fend for ourselves *and* our families.'

Douglas shook his head. He couldn't imagine his wife Cathie wanting to go out to work, not that he'd allow her to even if she did.

Jean heaved herself out of the car. It wasn't easy, and once again she told herself she really needed to lose some weight. But they'd had a lot of company at home over the holidays, with family visiting from Aberdeen, her brother from the USA, friends from all over the place. And, of course, one couldn't just sit there and watch one's guests eat by themselves.

'Douglas, let me know if anything else turns up, will you?' Jean wasn't quite sure what she meant, but she felt deeply distressed about Moira's death, and already had a nagging feeling that there was more to this case than a young mother suffering from depression and committing suicide.

Chapter Three

Douglas drove back to headquarters, preoccupied with thoughts about Moira Dalgleish. He didn't know much about her, except that she was well-known locally. Down at the river, Constable Jamieson, who was born in Perth and knew more about the inhabitants than Doug did, had muttered something to the effect that he'd heard that Moira Dalgleish had 'a bit of a reputation', at least before she went away to get married.

The very idea of having to interview the Dalgleish family put Doug's teeth on edge. Not that he had anything against the Dalgleishes; as far as he knew, they were perfectly nice people, aristocrats who had unfortunately come upon hard times. Alastair was the younger brother of Sir Colin Dalgleish, whom Doug had never seen and who was supposed to be rather strange and suffering from some nervous condition. Colin's wife, Lady Elspeth, was an anxious looking woman of about forty who wore no makeup and could occasionally be seen shopping in Perth, always dressed in a long, Dalgleish-tartan skirt. Sir Colin and Lady Elspeth lived in the rambling, run-down Dalgleish House, and Alastair and Patricia spent a good deal of time with them when Alastair wasn't in London or in his constituency near Edinburgh. Doug was thinking how little he knew about the Dalgleishes, as he pulled in to his parking space behind the headquarters building, although they were a household name in the area.

'I hear you've been out fishing, young fella.'

Detective Inspector Ian Garvie of the narcotics division appeared from nowhere and put one ham-like hand on the roof of Doug's car. He grinned. 'Did you find anything over the legal limit?'

'Aye, we did.' Douglas was not in a chatty mood, not even with his friend Ian. He couldn't get rid of the slimy feel of his hands and was aching to wash them. 'Nothing that would interest you, though.'

'They're an interesting bunch, the Dalgleishes,' went on Ian, accompanying Douglas into the building. 'I suppose a lot of those inbred old families are eccentric.'

'I thought that particular family was supposed to be pretty normal, aside from Sir Colin,' replied Douglas. He started up the concrete backstairs. 'For people who've never had to do a day's work in their lives, that is.' Douglas stopped off at the first-floor toilet to wash his hands.

'Oh, the Dalgleishes work hard enough,' said Ian rather vaguely. He stood in the doorway, waiting for Douglas to dry his hands. 'Do you know her? I mean Lady Elspeth?'

'Of course,' said Doug sarcastically. He pulled a set of keys out of his pocket and opened the door to his office. 'We spend our holidays in Capri with them – me and Cathie – then we go up to Balmoral for a spot of grouse shooting with the Duke of Edinburgh . . .'

'She was a Drummond before she married,' said Ian, following Doug into the tiny office. 'She used to be pretty, in a skinny kind of way; not too bright, though, and close to a breakdown since Sir Colin went off the deep end. She depends on Alastair a lot. He's the only one who's got any spunk or brains about him, but most of the time he's not there.'

'How do you happen to know so much about them?'

asked Doug. 'I've been in Perth just on six years now and, until a few days ago, I'd barely heard of them.'

'Six years!' said Ian pityingly. 'What do you think you can learn in six years? Maybe how to find your way around town, but not much more.'

Doug ignored the jibe. 'What do you know about Moira? Was she sane? Did she have enemies? Would anybody have killed her?' He sat back, challenging Ian to show how useful it was to have lived in Perth for four generations.

'Who said she was killed?' asked Ian, surprised. 'I heard on the scanner they were calling it an accidental drowning.'

'We'll know for sure tomorrow,' replied Doug. 'Meanwhile, there's no harm in keeping our ears open, is there?'

Jamieson appeared at the door, looking bedraggled. 'Can I go home to change, sir?' he asked Doug. He pulled at the knees of his dirty wet trousers to prove the necessity.

Doug eyed Jamieson up and down, and Garvie hid a smile. There was something comical about Jamieson's disgruntled and slightly resentful air, as if he held Doug responsible for his lamentable appearance.

'Yes, I suppose so, Jamieson,' said Doug after a pause. 'But first get Inspector Garvie and me a mug of coffee. Milk and two sugars for both, right?' He glanced at Ian, who nodded. Jamieson's wet boots slapped morosely down the corridor in the direction of the secretary's office and the coffee machine.

'Tell me some more about the Dalgleishes,' said Douglas.

'Well, there's Sir Colin, descended directly from Duncan Dalgleish, who took an active part in the Rising of 1715 where he was killed . . .'

Douglas was staring at Ian. 'Are you making this up? How could you know all that about them?'

'Lad, I was born and brought up here, and we take

our local gentry seriously. And this lot happens to be a big part of the history in this area. Anyway, old Duncan Dalgleish had a much younger brother, Glashan, a really bad character who had lost an eye from smallpox and was hideous from scars all over his face; he had a personality to match. Anyway, the brother not only betrayed Duncan to the English and thus indirectly caused his death, but after his brother died, he carried off one of Duncan's daughters away with him . . .'

'Ian, do you mind if we move up to the twentieth century, please? That's all very interesting, but I just need to know enough about the family to find out how and why Moira Dalgleish drowned.'

Ian sighed. It wasn't often that his interest in local history found an outlet in his work, and he had been enjoying the opportunity. 'Sir Colin is the eldest remaining of three brothers, the oldest of whom, Ian, was killed in a shooting accident near Ballater a few years back. Now *that* I know because I was a detective constable at the time, and we worked on the case.'

'Did anything come of it?' Douglas looked up.

'Nah. At first we thought there might be something, because there were just the two of them – Alastair and Ian – involved. But they seemed to get along well together, Alastair was very upset, and, of course, the title went to Colin, not to him. So it was clearly an accident. Every year a few people manage to get killed or badly injured during the shooting season.'

The phone rang and Doug picked it up. It was Malcolm Anderson, the pathologist.

'Dr Anderson? Aye, and a good morning to you, too. This one's a drowning, apparently, but, of course, there's always the possibility . . . Well, Malcolm, I'm sorry, I'm sure the woman wasn't aware of that, or she'd have done it differently . . .' Doug put his hand to the mouthpiece. 'Anderson says he doesn't like drownings,' he told Ian with a grin, then turned back to the phone. 'Will they do the post in Dundee or will you do it?'

'We've got permission to do it here,' replied Anderson. The main forensic pathology facility in Dundee was understaffed and their harassed pathologists were only too happy to shift some of their work into the capable hands of Malcolm Anderson.

'When?'

'As soon as we can. Maybe this afternoon. It doesn't sound like one we'd want to leave lying around too long, does it?' Dr Anderson laughed contentedly, and Douglas wondered what could make anyone want to become a pathologist. Certainly, Malcolm Anderson got his professional pleasures in ways that would make most people throw up.

'Could you let Dr Montrose know when you've settled on a time? She might want to be there.'

'Sure. It's always a pleasure to see her.'

Douglas put the phone down, shaking his head. Ian stood up. 'I'd better be getting back,' he said. 'Let me know if you need to know any more about the Dalgleishes.'

Chapter Four

Jean Montrose felt saddened and subdued by the time she walked up to her own front door and knocked the snow off her boots against the step. She brought in the milk and went into the kitchen. The house was very quiet, and the grey early morning light filtered reluctantly through the narrow window. A few minutes later a door opened upstairs, bare feet thudded on the carpeted floor, and a minute or two after that the toilet flushed. A new day had begun.

With a sigh, Jean went to the door that led down to the basement, where her two daughters had their bedrooms. It was easier that way; at Jean's insistence, the downstairs apartment had been redone for them, with a new bathroom, a tiny kitchen where they could make coffee and heat up pizzas, and one of the storage rooms had been converted into a living room where Fiona and Lisbie could entertain their friends without the sounds of laughter annoying Steven too much. Before, he had complained repeatedly about the noise they made in the living room. Now he had worried about what might be going on down there when he couldn't hear them.

'Fiona! Lisbie!' called Jean.

As usual, there was no answer, and Jean started down the narrow stairs, calling to them as she went. Usually,

by the time she got to the bottom, there would be groans
of response, but this morning there was only a stubborn
silence.

Fiona's room was first, and Jean opened the door and
switched on the light. A few weeks before, Fiona had
become tidy, almost obsessively so. Everything in the
room was in its place, her clothes and shoes neatly put
away, even her makeup, which she used to leave strewn
all over the floor, was carefully stored in a plastic case
on the dresser.

'Fiona, it's time to get up.' Jean looked at her watch.
It was almost eight o' clock, and her daughter would be
late for work if she didn't hurry up.

Fiona sat bolt upright in the bed, her dark hair
making a spiky halo around her pale, pretty face. 'I was
in the middle of a dream,' she said, rubbing her eyes.

'It's almost eight o' clock, dear,' said Jean firmly.

Fiona leapt out of bed in one bound. 'My God!' she
said, 'why didn't you tell me? There's a sales meeting
starting at half past.'

'The tea's ready upstairs,' replied Jean tranquilly.
'And you can take a buttery with you in the car. I'll
spread it with marmalade.'

While Fiona scrambled to get washed and dressed,
Jean went into the next room to wake Lisbie, who was a
sounder sleeper than her sister. After several minutes of
coaxing, Jean finally got her out of bed and pointed her
towards the bathroom, still half-asleep and mumbling.
Lisbie, a year younger than Fiona, was round and pretty
like her mother, with a little gap between her front teeth
that made her look younger than her age and somehow
naïve, but people thought that it added to her
attractiveness.

Half an hour later, Jean watched both girls as they
got ready to leave. She sighed a little bit enviously
looking at Fiona, who every morning managed
miraculously to transform herself from a pale, untidy,
ragged-looking waif to an elegantly turned-out executive.

Lisbie's car had broken down again, and Fiona agreed to give her a lift to the office, where she worked for a firm of Perth lawyers.

'Are you going to work dressed like that, Lisbie?' asked Fiona, her little nose crinkling with her usual early morning irritation. 'You look like the Michelin man after a big dinner.' Lisbie was wearing a thick white cable-knit sweater over her ordinary clothes and it did give her a somewhat spherical appearance.

'It's cold out there,' protested Lisbie. 'And anyway I don't care what you think. Alan likes me just the way I am.' She looked challengingly at her sister. 'He likes his women with some meat on them, that's what he says.'

Listening to her, Jean winced. Was that really the kind of thing that boys said to their girlfriends these days?

'It's a class thing,' said Fiona. 'The lower the class, the fatter the people.'

'He wouldn't even look at a bag of bones like you,' went on Lisbie contentedly, folding her napkin and putting it back in its ring, 'Except maybe to slip you a pound to buy yourself something to eat.'

Jean sighed. Usually there was a truce on working days, so that everyone could have breakfast in peace, and the girls' arguments didn't really get under way until they came home in the evening. Now Fiona's claws were coming out, and Jean interrupted her. 'All right, both of you, that's enough. You're late, so get going.' She looked at the clock and jumped up hurriedly. 'My goodness, I'm going to be late myself.'

Jean went up the stairs, balancing a cup of tea and a roll for Steven. As the manager of the Perth Glassworks, he didn't have to be at work at any specific time, but that didn't prevent him from complaining bitterly if he wasn't woken up. As it turned out, he was already awake.

'Here's your tea, dear,' said Jean. She put the cup down on the bedside table and went to draw back the curtains. Outside, Fiona's car was backing out of the short drive, the rear wheels slipping a little on the compacted snow and a plume of steamy white vapour coming from the exhaust. The cars parked on the other side of the street had a blanket of snow over them.

'What time is it?' asked Steven, sitting up.

'Almost half past eight,' replied Jean. 'Don't you have those Japanese buyers coming this morning?'

Steven drank his tea. 'They always give me a headache, those people,' he complained. 'I can never understand what they're talking about. They look at the merchandise, smile and bow and say, "All velly nice, Mr Montlose", and then they leave. I can never tell if they really like the product or if they're just being polite, not until I get an order, anyway.'

'Maybe you should learn to speak Japanese, Steven,' replied Jean, smiling. 'That would solve the problem, wouldn't it?'

Steven grunted. 'I don't have time for that,' he said dismissively. 'I have far too many other things to do.'

'There's more tea in the pot,' said Jean, and I've left the butteries out on the table. I have to go now.'

She gave Steven an affectionate kiss before going back downstairs to get her coat.

Jean didn't like driving in snow, and she crept down the hill in first gear, hunched over the steering wheel, all thoughts out of her mind until she parked her car on the corner next to the surgery, behind her partner Helen Inkster's new grey Vauxhall.

When Jean came up the path, sliding on the hardened snow, she saw Eleanor, their secretary, muffled up in a coat and tartan scarf, pushing ineffectively at the snow with a shovel outside the door.

'This is a job for a man,' puffed Eleanor, leaning against the shovel and wheezing. She was flabby, overweight and never did any exercise. 'And anyway, shovelling snow isn't in my job description.'

'Right,' said Jean briskly. 'You go inside and do your work. I'll take care of this.'

Eleanor didn't hesitate, although she turned at the door to tell Jean that she had some patients in the waiting room.

Five minutes later, Jean had cleared a narrow path down to the gate, but she, too, was wheezing and out of breath. By the time she had come in, taken her coat off and sat down, her face was red and she was still puffing.

Helen came into Jean's office. A big, cheerful woman, Helen never wore makeup on her ruddy, healthy face, and liked sensible tweeds and stout walking-shoes. Helen had a direct, uncompromising manner that didn't always sit well with the patients, who often preferred Jean's gentler and more understanding approach. Helen had played hockey for St Andrews, come out near the top of her medical-school class, and was professionally well regarded by her colleagues.

'I told Eleanor to clear the path. If I'd known you were going to take over, I'd have done it myself.'

'You shouldn't even think of doing it,' said Jean. Helen had recently had a lot of trouble with her back, and Jean was seriously concerned about her partner's health. 'Anyway, Eleanor would have whined about it all day,' Jean went on, still puffing slightly. 'It was easier to do it myself.'

'Eleanor told me they'd found poor Moira Dalgleish drowned in the Tay.' Helen put a sturdy foot up on the patients' chair. 'That's going to cause a stir in society circles . . .' Helen's eyes didn't leave Jean's ' . . . and elsewhere too, I suppose.'

'Elsewhere?' she asked.

'They say she was pretty free with her favours before she married,' said Helen. 'That's just hearsay, of course. She seemed a very nice young woman when I met her.'

'She was.' Jean never liked to think or speak ill of

anyone, and felt defensive about Moira, whom she had known as an intelligent, attractive, out-going woman with a lovely personality and a lot of character. If Moira had chosen to have an active social life before her marriage that was her privilege and nobody else's business. 'It's a real tragedy for her baby, too,' went on Jean. 'First his father dead, and now his mother. I suppose Lady Dalgleish will take care of him. I don't know much about the rest of their family, do you?'

'Just what everybody knows. Did you know Lady Elspeth is coming to see you this morning? She's on the surgery list, or her grandson is, anyway. Denys Dalgleish Glashan.'

'Oh dear,' said Jean. 'Poor little Denys. It's such a big name for that wee child. And it's confusing, because Moira had gone back to using her maiden name. I hope there's nothing the matter with him.'

'It seems odd that Elspeth would bring him in on the very day her daughter was found drowned,' said Helen.

'I think Denys is due to have his vaccinations,' said Jean, but she couldn't help agreeing with Helen.

Ten minutes later, Lady Elspeth came into Jean's office, wearing a long tartan skirt, the hem of which hung over a pair of old but well-kept boots. She was holding Denys to her as if she were scared of dropping him.

'Here's the young man,' she said, smiling nervously at Jean. 'He's all ready for his immunization, or whatever you call it.'

Jean took the child and put him on the examining table. He was a fine-looking boy of about six months, making contented gurgling noises as he lay on his back. Normally, the mothers would undress their babies for examination, which gave Jean an opportunity to chat with them about any problems they were having. It became immediately obvious that Elspeth either didn't know how to or didn't want to undress her grandson, so

Jean expertly undressed him and took off his nappy herself.

'He's already starting to stand up in his crib,' said Elspeth.

Jean checked Denys's chubby legs. He was kicking vigorously, and the soles of his feet were losing their rounded contour, perhaps even a little ahead of schedule.

'All the male Dalgleishes have that,' said Elspeth, who was watching Jean examine Denys's toes. The fourth and fifth toes on each side were fused together, a minor congenital abnormality.

'I know,' said Jean, 'I made a note of it when I first saw him.' She watched Elspeth to see how much of this she understood. 'Being a Dalgleish, I suppose you know it's congenital, linked to the paternal Y chromosome?'

'I'm sure you're right,' Elspeth tried to smile, 'but I don't understand any of that medical talk. You must see a lot of that kind of thing in old families,' she went on, her eyes bright and anxious. 'Thinned-out blood, I suppose. Anyway, thank God, Denys doesn't have haemophilia or anything like that.' She was speaking fast and nervously, and Jean thought she looked close to the end of her tether.

'He's perfectly normal,' said Jean in a reassuring voice. 'Moira was very concerned about these things too, so we checked everything. There's nothing to worry about.'

'Poor Moira,' said Elspeth, turning her head away when Jean stuck the needle into Denys's little bottom. 'Patricia told me you were down at the river with the police last night. Do you have any idea about . . . about what might have happened?' There was a tremor in her voice, but to Jean it didn't quite ring the right note.

'You'd have to ask Inspector Niven,' replied Jean. 'The only reason I was there was because she had been my patient and the police surgeon wasn't available.'

'When will they know?' Elspeth went on. 'I suppose
they'll . . . examine her body, won't they?' There was
an anxiety surfacing in Elspeth's voice that Jean
couldn't understand. Surely she knew that all drowning
victims were autopsied; sometimes it wasn't easy to tell
if they had died before or after going into the water.

'I imagine they'll be doing it some time today.'

The door opened and Eleanor poked her head into the
room without knocking. 'That was Dr Anderson on the
phone,' she said, glancing curiously at Elspeth. 'He says
they're starting in an hour, and he'd be glad if you could
be there.'

Jean flushed with annoyance at Eleanor's lack of
discretion, but there wasn't much she could do at that
moment.

'There's your answer,' she said when Eleanor had
withdrawn.

'Will you let me know what they find?' asked
Elspeth, gingerly picking up her grandson.

'I'm sorry, Elspeth, but I can't discuss the findings
with anyone,' replied Jean, astonished by Elspeth's
request. 'It's a police matter and none of my business,
really. I'm sure that Inspector Niven would be able to
tell you at some point, or perhaps it would be easier if
you asked your solicitor to contact him.'

'Thank you, Dr Montrose,' said Elspeth formally.
She seemed to be hesitating. She put the child down for
a moment. 'Jean, there's been a lot happening in the last
few weeks; things I don't know if I have to tell the police
about. I wonder if we could talk, just you and I, woman
to woman?'

Jean looked at the clock. 'I simply can't now,
Elspeth. I have patients out there that I have to see . . .'

'Oh, I didn't mean now,' said Elspeth hurriedly.
'Maybe we could meet for coffee, or you could come up
to the house. That might be better, because that's
where . . .' Elspeth caught herself, and looked
enquiringly at Jean, who suppressed a sigh. She was

really too busy to get involved with this, but she could feel her curiosity getting the better of her.

'All right,' said Jean. 'Maybe this coming weekend? I'm not working on Sunday.'

'That would be perfect, thank you so much, Jean. Come at about eleven, if that's convenient, and we'll have time for a chat. Bring your family; we're having a few people over, and there'll be some young people their age.' There were unexpected bright tears in Elspeth's eyes, and she was still hesitating about something; Jean feeling a vast sympathy for this frail-looking woman who had lost her daughter and who seemed to have a problem just coping, stood up and gave her a big, motherly hug.

Elspeth reached into her handbag and pulled out a small leather-covered book. 'This is Moira's,' she said, handing it to Jean, who looked at it in astonishment. 'It's her address and appointment book. I, well, I just didn't feel it was right to leave it lying around, and I thought . . .' Elspeth sounded confused and unsure of herself, and tears were forming in her eyes again.

'I can keep it here for you if you like, Elspeth,' said Jean doubtfully, 'but . . .'

'It's just that I want it out of the way,' said Elspeth, 'and I didn't know what to do with it.'

Jean put it in the desk drawer, which was already almost full of various drug samples.

Elspeth left with her grandson, leaving Jean wondering why she had really come, and whether her nervousness had anything to do with Moira's death, or whether it was from other reasons.

Chapter Five

The telecommunications people had traced the call to a phone-box in one of the poorer outlying areas of Perth, and there the trail stopped. Douglas Niven went down with a couple of his men to the basement room at headquarters where the sound equipment was kept, and listened several times to the brief segment of tape. Somebody suggested it might be a man disguising his voice, but to the others it was pretty clear that the voice was female, although there was a huskiness that might have been caused by a handkerchief placed over the mouthpiece.

'That wasn't just an innocent bystander calling in,' said Jamieson in his portentous way. 'Or why would they bother to disguise their voice or not say who they were?'

As usual, the others ignored him.

'Let's see,' said Douglas, checking the label on the cassette. 'The call came in at four thirty-two a.m. What was the woman doing at an outdoor phone-box at that time in the morning? Why would she have been at the river, on a bitterly cold night, when snow had been falling?'

'An early-morning dip, perhaps?' suggested Bob, the audiovisual technician, a slender, long-haired young man whose face and neck were beset by angry red pustules of acne.

His frivolous comment brought him a frosty glare from Douglas. 'When I want your opinion, sonny, I'll ask for it,' he told him sternly. 'Meanwhile, don't chip in with the grown-ups, all right?'

Doug turned to the others. 'Doesn't it suggest that maybe the woman was involved in some way?'

Ian Garvie, who had been in the basement when Doug and Jamieson came down, and had stayed out of curiosity, asked rather diffidently if they knew for sure that they had a crime to investigate.

Doug scratched his head. 'I don't know. But this was a strange phone call, wouldn't you say? We get drownings every so often, but the bodies are usually found by fishermen or people taking a walk along the river, or by divers if the victim was seen jumping.'

Jamieson was looking blank, and Ian didn't seem to know what Doug was getting at, so he went on. 'In other words, it's not a surprise if a *drowning* is a mystery, but this is the first time in my experience that the *finding* of the body has turned out to be even more mysterious.'

'Have you talked to the Dalgleishes yet?' asked Ian. 'Maybe one of them, or a bailiff, might have seen something and phoned in.'

'I don't believe they have any female bailiffs at the Dalgleishes',' said Doug heavily. 'And even if they did, why wouldn't they tell us who they were?'

'Maybe we can get some fingerprints off the phone,' suggested Jamieson.

Doug shrugged. 'Maybe. But let's wait until after the post-mortem,' he said. 'If this turns out to be just an ordinary accidental drowning, we have better things to do with our time than to investigate a non-crime.'

Douglas was feeling edgy, and it showed. He was fervently hoping that Moira Dalgleish had tripped and fallen into the river, because right now he didn't need a big criminal investigation on his hands. Cathie was going to have the baby soon, and she needed a lot of support and attention, and aside from that he had plenty of other work to do. And at the back of his mind was the hope that he could avoid interviewing the aristocratic Dalgleish family.

As the matter involved such well-known people, Douglas decided to discuss it with his direct superior, Chief Inspector Bob McLeod. Bob was in his office on the third floor. He was stocky, grizzled, and sitting, as usual, behind a pile of papers a foot high, spread out all over his desk. Doug wondered how he ever found anything; it was common knowledge that the secretaries regarded working for him as equivalent to being sent to Siberia. Bob was smoking his pipe. Whether or not he did it knowingly nobody knew for sure, but the way he puffed on it usually gave a good indication of his state of mind. Now the air was thick with smoke and it kept coming out of the pipe in swift, half-intermitted bursts: a sure sign that Bob was not happy.

He looked up when Doug came in.

'I just had Chief Constable McConnach on the phone,' he said. 'And before him it was Superintendent Walsh.' Bob pointed the stem of his pipe at Douglas. 'We have instructions to deal with this morning's drowning with "discretion and despatch". You know what that means?'

'Yes, sir,' replied Doug.

'That means quick results and no comment to the papers, the TV, anybody, OK, Niven? And that goes double for Jamieson. I seem to remember he got us some unwanted publicity a few months ago. Talk to him, all right?'

'Yes, sir.'

Bob leaned forward. 'Doug, we have to go very carefully on this one. Somebody high in the Scottish Office phoned McConnach first thing this morning about it, so he's got everybody all hot and bothered.

Just pray there wasna foul play in this case, then we won't need to get any more involved.'

Doug moved his feet. 'Yes, sir.'

'When's the post-mortem?'

'Sometime today, I believe, sir.'

'Be there. Let me know the minute you have any new information.'

'Yes, sir.'

Bob nodded, and went back to his papers.

Outside, Douglas grinned at the secretary, a pale young woman with short blonde hair and glasses which didn't hide her slight squint. She had a tall pile of papers on her desk and didn't look any happier than Bob.

Driving to the hospital pathology department, where the autopsy was to be carried out, Douglas wondered about Bob's warning. There was something odd about all the high-level attention the case was getting; in his experience, the more the high-ups tried to cover up a case, the more attention it would get when the media realized, as they always did, that somebody was trying to hide information from them. Doug could have told these officials that the most effective way to suppress information was to let the investigation go forward normally and then lose or ignore the results.

The snow was starting to fall again, and Doug turned on the windscreen wipers, but they left a blind area. He didn't see the ambulance coming out through the hospital gates and only the fast reflexes of the driver avoided what could have been a serious accident.

The pathology department was located down a long corridor next to the old hospital laundry, which now served as a storage area for unused beds, medical equipment and linen. The heavy, spring-loaded door closed after Douglas, and, as always, he felt that the gates of hell had shut behind him. Attending autopsies had never been his favourite way of spending a morning, although he had been to enough of them to know that he wouldn't faint or otherwise disgrace himself.

The corridor was narrow, and illuminated by a series of bare light-bulbs strung between a maze of electrical cables and conduits of different sizes, each covered with thick flaking white paint and fragmenting insulation.

The outside-door opened and closed behind him, letting a momentary shaft of daylight into the corridor, and he heard a familiar voice call out. 'Douglas!'

He waited while Jean came up. She was dressed in a thick woolly black coat and snow boots, and looked like a teddy bear.

'I hate this place,' she said, half to herself, as they stopped outside the door of the pathology department. Douglas rang the bell at the side of a red-on-white sign that said 'Pathology Department. Authorized personnel ONLY.'

'Me too,' confessed Doug. 'Can you imagine spending your life doing this kind of thing?'

The intercom crackled, and Doug announced himself and Jean. 'Push the door when you hear the buzzer.' Jean recognized the voice of Brian Thomson, the technician. They went in, past a series of tiny offices and rooms with shelves up to the ceiling, loaded with glass jars containing various human organs, brown with age and formalin. Just outside the double doors of the autopsy room was a small table with a coffee machine, a box containing little packets of sugar and milk-substitute, and a stack of styrofoam cups. Jean felt revolted by the idea of eating or drinking anything so close to a place where dead bodies were broken down into their component parts, but Doug didn't seem to give it a thought, and poured himself a coffee. A red light-bulb glowed above the double doors, indicating that the room was in use.

Malcolm Anderson came out wearing a mask. 'This one's a real stinker,' he said cheerfully. 'Come on in.'

He looked at Jean. 'Are you sure you want to do this, quine?' he asked, in a concerned tone of voice.

'Well, I didn't come here just to sit and wait for you to finish,' replied Jean bravely, although she already felt that she might have made a mistake in coming. The stench from inside the autopsy room was percolating through the entire department.

'All right then,' said Dr Anderson. 'Leave your coats out here and put on gowns. They're over here in a pile. One size fits all.'

Once gowned, Jean and Douglas each took a paper mask from a box outside the door and followed Dr Anderson into the long, well-lit room. He indicated several pairs of long-sleeved red rubber-gloves hanging from a wooden rack near the door, but as neither Douglas nor Jean had any intention of handling the body or any part of it, they ignored his offer.

Brian Thomson was standing near the body, apparently unmoved by the appalling smell emanating from it. Moira was still wearing the clothes she had been found in, a once-bright flower-patterned cotton dress, now encrusted with mud, and split by the swelling and distension of the abdomen. Her pale, swollen arms were sticking out at an angle from the body, and where Jamieson had pulled on it, the skin had torn and slid down below the elbow, forming wrinkled folds like a thick sock.

'No coat,' said Douglas, although he had noticed that fact when Moira was pulled out of the water. The door opened again and Jamieson came in, wrinkling his nose in disgust.

'Get a mask,' Douglas told him, although he knew from personal experience that the paper fabric did nothing to filter out the smell.

'No coat,' he repeated. 'I can't imagine her walking along the river dressed like that.'

Malcolm Anderson went up to the body and rather gingerly moved it over on its side. The body moved loosely, as if it were about to fall apart. Near the armpit, both Jean and Douglas saw a flash of silver.

'Take it out, Brian,' said Dr Anderson.

'Use forceps,' cautioned Douglas. 'There might be some prints on it.'

Brian grasped the object with a Kelly clamp and freed it with a pair of scissors. Silently he held it out for their examination. It was a slightly concave object about the size and shape of a teaspoon. Attached to one end by a short series of metal links was a triple hook, and at the other end, a broken piece of blue nylon line a few inches long.

'Biggest fish anybody ever got in the Tay, I'd guess,' said Dr Anderson grinning. Carefully, he eased the body back into its original position.

Douglas took a small plastic bag out of his jacket pocket and held it open for Brian to drop the lure into it, hooks first. Doug was careful not to touch the shiny surface.

'OK, you can cut the clothes off now,' Dr Anderson said to Brian. 'I suppose you'll need them?' he asked Douglas, who nodded without enthusiasm.

'Write a time and place label for this,' said Douglas, handing the plastic bag to Jamieson. 'Then take it to the lab. I didn't see anything, but they might get some latent prints off it.'

Jamieson took it. His usually ruddy face was grey, and in some way the unaccustomed pallor accentuated his bulk. Jean glanced at him and imagined the earth-shaking thud he would make if he fainted and fell on the floor.

Thankfully, Jamieson turned away and went over to a small desk near the door to write the label.

With the clothes cut and removed, Moira Dalgleish was a distended, bloated and repulsive sight, but Jean felt only a profound sorrow that this unfortunate young woman, who by rights had so many years of happy and healthy life ahead of her, should have come to such a

sad end. She wondered what could possibly have
happened. Moira had not been particularly big or
strong, but could have given an assailant a hard battle if
she were fighting for her life. But then, Jean reminded
herself, she might have been knocked out first, or had a
sudden episode of disorientation, walked out of the
house in that light attire, and fallen down the river
bank, made treacherous by the ice and snow.

Brian opened the abdomen with a large knife, and
they all heard, then a moment later smelled, the escape
of foul, putrefied air from the abdominal cavity. The
intestines and internal organs were partly liquefied,
which made removing them intact an almost impossible
task.

They were gathered around the partly eviscerated
body when they all saw a sudden, slithery movement
inside the belly. Jamieson stepped back with a hoarse
shout, his eyes protruding. Jean, thinking she might
have imagined it, watched, almost hypnotized. When
the movement occurred again, deep inside the dead
woman's abdomen, Jean thought she was going to
faint. Douglas started to sweat and he too backed away
from the table.

Dr Anderson reached in with his red-gloved hand and
pulled out a squirming, slithering object about a foot
long. 'Freshwater eel,' he said, brandishing the creature
above his head. 'I haven't seen one of those for a while,
not here anyway. Most interesting . . .' He held the eel
at eye level as it tried to wriggle out of his grasp. 'They
creep in through the anus, did you know that, Douglas?
They can work their way all the way up the intestine,
although I've never actually seen that. In fact, a few
years ago, a Dr Grutzenbach in Vienna wrote a paper
pointing out that you could get a rough estimate of the
time of death from the distance the creature had
travelled. I can get you a reprint if you like . . .'

There was a gurgling noise behind them, and Dr
Anderson stopped talking and turned around,

astonished. Jamieson was leaning over one of the stainless steel sinks and vomiting noisily, as if his own entire insides were coming up.

Jean went over to assist him, but he gave her such a baleful, red-eyed glare that she left him to his own devices.

'All right, Jamieson, pull yourself together,' snapped Douglas, who a moment before had been a hair's breadth from suffering the same gastric contractions. 'Maybe you should have joined the Girl Guides rather than the Tayside Police Force.'

'Yes, sir,' replied Jamieson, turning to face his superior. He wiped a fleck of saliva from his chin with the back of his sleeve. 'It must have been something I ate,' he mumbled, taking care not to look at Jean.

Without a word, Brian came over and turned the water full on in the sink. It wasn't the first time that visitors had vomited into it.

For the next ten minutes or so, neither Douglas nor Jean could bring themselves to approach the body, and they talked in whispers while Dr Anderson and Brian worked. A few minutes after they started dissecting the neck, Dr Anderson turned to face them.

'Come over here!' he exclaimed, his voice vibrant with excitement. 'Look at this!'

He showed them the fractured hyoid bone in the neck. That proved conclusively, he told them, holding up the specimen for their inspection, that Moira Dalgleish had been manually strangled before being thrown into the water. 'Thumbs,' said Malcolm, pointing to the fracture with his forceps.

'Any indication of who might have done it? Male or female?' asked Doug.

'She was a healthy, strong young woman, wasn't she? That means that it was probably a man, unless she was taken by surprise or asleep. Even then, that would be unlikely, unless you believe the kind of rubbish you read in those P.D. James murder stories.'

She turned back to Dr Anderson. 'Was there any other injury, like a skull fracture, Malcolm?' she asked. 'I once heard of a fractured hyoid being the result of other direct injuries, and not from strangling.'

There was a long pause, while Dr Anderson surveyed Jean with a curious expression. Finally, he pointed at the small high window through which they had a restricted view of a couple of leafless trees at the edge of the hospital car-park.

'You see that bird, quine?' he said to Jean. Astonished, Jean followed his finger, and sure enough there was a small bird sitting on the end of a branch.

'Yes, Malcolm, but what—'

'What kind is it?' he asked brusquely.

'I don't know,' replied Jean smiling. 'I suppose it could be a sparrow or maybe a starling . . .'

'I don't know what kind it is either, quine,' said Malcolm. 'But we can be pretty sure it's no' a bird of paradise, right?'

They all stared at him.

'What I mean,' said Malcolm patiently, 'is that in nine hundred and ninety-nine cases out of a thousand fractured hyoids, manual strangulation is the cause. On the thousandth case, well maybe a bird of paradise did it.'

Chapter Six

The fingerprint analysts got a partial index and maybe a smeared third from the metal lure, hardly enough to put into the central computer searching system, but, according to Sergeant Foster, the man in charge, probably enough for a positive identification if they had a good set to compare them with.

Sergeant Foster leaned back in his chair; brawny and shirt-sleeved, looking complacent, as if he'd just completed an outstanding and difficult job.

'You're done with it?' Doug asked, surprised that the lure had remained shiny through all its sinister travels.

Foster shrugged. 'Why? Was there something else you wanted us to do with it?' He sounded disgruntled, as if he'd been expecting a compliment.

Doug picked the lure up, taking care not to touch the hooks, and put it back in its plastic bag.

'Sign the item out in the book, please.' Sergeant Foster pushed the hardcovered ledger towards Doug, who signed it, thus confirming that he had taken possession of item No.466/90676, which might at some later date be used as evidence in court.

Doug drove out to the Dalgleish estate, through a side entrance on to a narrow road. A snowplough had been down recently and left a track just wide enough for Douglas's car. After about a quarter of a mile the road divided, one branch turning right towards the main house, which Doug could glimpse in his rear-view mirror as a long façade of grey granite. Doug took the left-hand fork which sloped gently down for a hundred yards until he came to a small cluster of rough-granite buildings, typical Scottish workers' one-storied cottages, with sloping slate-roofs and a central doorway with a window on either side. A large barn, converted into a garage, stood to one side, accessible from the road. The snow was undisturbed except for a few foot-tracks leading to the cottages. Withered, black grass stems, remnants of the past season, poked through the snow.

Douglas had been here before. Kevin Marshall, the bailiff, lived with his wife in the cottage nearest the road, and the last one, closer to the river that flowed some twenty yards beyond a wide row of tall trees, was home to Emily, the Dalgleishes' cook and housekeeper. The third cottage had remained empty since its last occupant left.

Douglas saw Kevin Marshall trudging towards him from the direction of Dalgleish House. Tall, thick-necked, heavily built, with a pot-belly that had fooled the occasional poacher into thinking that Kevin couldn't move fast, he recognized Douglas but made no sign. He kept up the same pace until he was within a few yards of the inspector, then stopped.

'Aye,' said Doug after a pause.

'Aye, yersel',' replied Kevin, watching Douglas with small, narrowed eyes.

'How's the fishing?' asked Douglas.

'You'd know better than me about that, from what I hear.' Kevin didn't crack a grin, but the atmosphere between them was comfortable enough. They knew each other slightly, but like most local citizens, Kevin didn't care for the police to be calling in his home territory.

'D'you have a minute?' asked Douglas.

Kevin shrugged. Douglas took the plastic bag out of

his pocket. 'Ever seen one of these? ' he asked, holding it out. Kevin came forward to look at it. He didn't touch the bag.

'It looks like a spoon lure,' he said.

'Right,' said Douglas. 'Anybody around here use them?'

'Occasionally.'

'Anybody in particular like to use them, that you know of?'

Kevin shook his head, but his eyes were thoughtful. 'No. It depends on the season, the weather, that sort of thing, I suppose.'

'You know that Miss Moira was found just a little way down the river,' said Doug in a matter-of-fact way, using the name that she was always called by on the estate and around town.

Kevin nodded. 'About a half-mile,' he said.

Douglas leaned forward confidentially. 'We're dealing with a murder here, Kevin.'

There was a shocked silence for a moment.

'Who'd want to kill her? She was never . . . She wasn't one to hurt anybody. And she has that wee baby.'

'That's what we're trying to find out,' replied Douglas. 'Now, about that lure . . .'

'Well, you know we get poachers around here quite a bit.'

'Aye, I'm aware of that, Kevin, but I thought they used lamps and explosives nowadays.'

'They do indeed,' said Kevin, his lips tightening with disgust. 'Most of them, that is.'

Douglas waited while Kevin struggled with his natural tendency never to tell a policeman anything he didn't know already.

Kevin started to walk past Douglas towards his cottage. After he'd taken a few steps, he half-turned his head and said, 'You might want to ask Rory McDermott about that lure.' He hesitated, and shuffled his feet. His eyes flickered again over Doug's shoulder at the cottages. 'You know Rory used to work for us as a ghillie, don't you? He lived in that cottage.' Kevin pointed to the empty building. He hesitated. 'You know there was a big fuss with him, up at the house.'

There must have been a movement behind a curtain, because Kevin said in a low voice, 'Maggie's watching. She doesn't like the police.' He pronounced it *po-liss*.

'That's all right,' said Doug. 'I need to talk to Maggie for a minute anyway.'

Kevin didn't answer, and plodded on, striking a course through the fresh snow over to his cottage. Doug followed him.

Maggie looked a good fifteen years older than Kevin, which would make her somewhere around sixty. She had lost her teeth and chewed continually on her gums, making her chin move up and down like a piston.

Maggie did not appear delighted to see Kevin, and even less to see Doug. 'I ain't got nothing to tell you,' she said.

Doug, not entirely unused to this kind of response, sat down on a wooden chair while Kevin went into the bedroom to take off his boots.

It turned out that Kevin and Maggie had both been away visiting her sister in Arbroath at the time Moira disappeared, so there was little they could tell Douglas about the events around the time of the murder. 'Rory McDermott used to live next door, right?' he asked, changing tack.

'Him and Bella,' said Maggie.

'Did Bella work up at the house, too?' Douglas's voice was noncommittal.

'She used to,' replied Maggie. 'Why don't you ask her? It's none of my business. Or yours either,' she added as an aside.

Douglas tried for another few minutes, but by the time he left, he had elicited nothing of any value from them. He decided to leave his car where it was; walking the half-mile up to the big house would give him time to think about Rory McDermott, whom he'd heard of but never met, and also time to work himself up for the unpleasant task of interviewing the Dalgleishes.

By the time her afternoon surgery was finished, Jean was exhausted. Some days it seemed that all she saw in the surgery were children, and today, there had been an invasion of them. All afternoon, howling boys and girls had filled the surgery, some with earaches, others with colds, others who just seemed to enjoy howling.

Jean, finally able to sit down, felt the sadness and anxiety about Moira flooding back. She remembered the little address and appointments book Elspeth had given her, and, resisting the temptation to open it, put it in her bag to take home and give to Douglas next time she saw him.

Helen came into Jean's office, tense and tight-lipped after dealing with her share of the children. 'How would it be if we separated off the paediatric part of the practice, Jean?' she asked, flopping down into the patient's chair. 'You could be in charge of it, and take care of these little monsters all by yourself.'

Jean pushed her chair away from her desk. 'Do you still have that bottle of sherry?' she asked, her eyes lighting up. 'If there's one time I could really use a drink, it's now.'

Helen stood up and went to the door. 'That's the best idea I've heard all week,' she said. 'Get us a couple of glasses from the lab, and we're all set.'

Two minutes later, they were sitting down, each holding a small glass of Dry Sack. Helen had put the jute-bagged bottle on the middle of Jean's desk.

Eleanor came in, and disapproval spread across her face when she saw the evidence of the debauchery she had long suspected.

'What do you want, Eleanor?' snapped Helen. 'Don't you know you're supposed to knock before coming in to our offices?'

'I'm sorry,' said Eleanor, looking crestfallen and annoyed at the same time. She was always careful to knock at Helen's door, but usually didn't bother when she came into Jean's. 'They just called from the nursing home,' she went on, addressing Jean, a smug tone in her voice. 'They said your mother's packed all her things and says she's ready to go home.'

Jean sighed. 'Tell them I'll be over in half an hour,' she said. 'Meanwhile,' she paused, and glanced at Helen, 'tell them to give her an extra glass of sherry. That always seems to calm her down.'

Eleanor hesitated, obviously aghast at the suggestion, then saw Helen's eyebrows coming together in a threatening frown, so she scurried out of the office, shuffling her flat feet.

'You just have to be more firm with her,' said Helen when the door closed. She shrugged her shoulders. 'Once you make it clear who's the boss, all you need to do is say "jump", and she'll ask you how high.'

'Maybe that's all *you* need to say,' replied Jean, who knew that once a relationship was solidly established, there was very little that could be done to change it. 'If *I* ever said "jump" to her, she'd jump all right, straight down my throat.'

'You were going to tell me about the post-mortem on Moira Dalgleish,' said Helen, sitting back and stretching out her solid, thick-stockinged legs in front of her. She raised her glass to her lips, watching Jean attentively.

'I don't remember saying anything of the sort,' retorted Jean, still put out by Eleanor's visible lack of respect for her, and the contrasting deference with which she treated Helen.

'It's my guess that she was murdered,' said Helen, eyeing Jean for clues. 'She was perfectly sane, and a very good swimmer.'

'How do you happen to know that?' asked Jean, astonished. Everybody seemed to know more about the

Dalgleishes than she did. Even Douglas Niven had been telling her details about their history when they were leaving the hospital after the autopsy, and he'd only been in Perth for a few years. Doug had admitted that most of his information came from Inspector Ian Garvie, a passionate local historian.

'A few years ago, I had to certify that she was healthy enough to be on her school swimming-team,' replied Helen. 'So even if she did happen to be gallivanting down by the river in a summer dress in the middle of the night and fell in, she could easily have swum back to the shore.'

'That's true, unless she jumped in on purpose to commit suicide,' said Jean. 'Actually, aside from an adventurous eel, the only useful thing Dr Anderson found at the post-mortem was a fractured hyoid.'

'So she was strangled,' said Helen, her big grey eyes round with interest, 'There's no other way the hyoid can be broken, is there?'

'That's more or less what Dr Anderson said,' replied Jean.

'What about the eel?' asked Helen, puzzled, then added hurriedly, 'Don't tell me; I'm quite certain it's some disgusting detail that would give me nightmares for weeks. Jean, how on earth can you deal with all these horrible things you seem to get involved in all the time?'

'It's a combination of an iron stomach and a total lack of imagination,' replied Jean, but her voice was flat and distant, and she was quite obviously thinking about something else.

After a loud and emphatic knock on the door, Eleanor came back in, a triumphant look on her face. 'I gave them your message, Doctor Montrose,' she said. 'About giving your mother another glass of sherry.'

'Well?' asked Jean after a pause.

'Mrs Findlay has already had some,' answered Eleanor, crossing her hands in front of her chest. 'In fact, the nurse said that she apparently consumed most of an entire bottle of Tio Peep this afternoon.'

'That particular brand happens to be called *Tio Pépé*,' snapped Helen.

'Whatever,' said Eleanor, staring with some satisfaction at Jean. 'Anyway, the nurse said that your mother's as drunk as a skunk and she'd like you to come out there as soon as you can.'

Chapter Seven

Douglas plodded towards Dalgleish House. The paths had not been cleared, although several people, both male and female, judging by the footprints, had travelled in both directions since the last snowfall. A breeze stirred high above him in the trees, and fat clumps of snow fell from the branches on to the ground around him. As he approached the back of the sprawling house, Douglas could feel an almost palpable sadness, a desolation, about the place. A dog barked, a deep sound followed by another, and Doug wondered a little nervously if they had guard dogs on the loose. A seven-foot brick wall, crudely harled over, surrounded what Douglas assumed to be the kitchen garden. A wooden gate stood solidly in the middle of the wall, shedding flakes of faded green paint. He poked a finger at the round bellpush, but from the stiff, unused feel of it he was sure that it had no functioning electrical connections within the house.

He was about to walk around to the main entrance when it occurred to him to give the door a push. It opened on to a straight path leading through a bleak, snow-covered garden with a few collapsed remnants of greenery, and on his right, an irregular row of slender stakes that must have supported last year's peas or beans. Beyond that, a wire fence kept a dozen chickens from wandering through the garden. Doug walked towards the house, keeping an eye out for the dogs, which, to judge by the suddenly excited barking, seemed to have heard him although they were still not visible.

The kitchen door opened and a large, raw-boned, middle-aged muscular woman came out, carrying a green plastic rubbish bag. She almost dropped the bag with surprise when she saw Doug.

'Who are you?' she asked. Her voice was deep and she stood threateningly, feet apart in a fighter's stance. 'This is private property.'

'It's all right, ma'am,' said Douglas, smiling reassuringly. 'I'm a police officer. I just cut through here rather than walking all the way round to the front.'

The woman didn't sound particularly impressed. 'I can guess what you're here about,' she said, her voice still sharp. 'You'd better talk to Mr Alastair. He should be up in his office. You wait right there, and I'll take you up in a minute.' She took the heavy plastic bag over to a large container and lifted the lid.

'Here,' said Douglas, following her, 'let me do that.'

'Get away from me,' said the woman threateningly, and Douglas backed off.

When she had disposed of the rubbish, she cocked her finger at Douglas, and he followed her through the kitchen, a big, low-ceilinged, whitewashed room with a slate floor and a single window facing the garden. There was a huge, old-fashioned iron range with two large black pots against the long wall, and a line of modern steel-and-brass pans hung on the wall next to it. The opposite wall was lined by wooden cupboards that reached up to the ceiling. A wide hatch beyond the cupboards held stacks of plates and cutlery, evidently in readiness to be sent up to the dining room. Doug was conscious of the noise his shoes made on the floor.

'What's your name?' he asked.

'Emily McNab,' the woman replied, without turning round.

'I may need to come back and talk to you,' he said.

'Well, you'll be wasting your time.' Her voice was sharp again. 'I don't know nothing about what goes on upstairs.'

She opened a door that led to a wooden stairway with worn dark-red carpeting, and went up with a determined, foot-slapping walk. Douglas had to hurry to keep up with her.

The door at the top of the stairs, bigger and more ornate than the one below, opened into the corner of a long oak-panelled hallway. Perhaps it was the contrast between the rather cramped quarters downstairs, but the hall had a barn-like stillness about it. There was not much in the way of decoration; an ancient brass candelabrum, large but not ornate, hung over the centre of the hall, and various thick external wires showed that at some time it had been rather clumsily converted from candles to electricity.

'Oh, excuse me, sir!' Emily stepped forward and almost bumped into a figure who was heading for the great staircase.

'No harm done, Emily.' Douglas recognized the man as Alastair Dalgleish; this was the first time he'd had a close look at him. Alastair was in his forties, good-looking, with a thick but well-groomed moustache. He was tall, well-dressed in what Douglas recognized to be an expensive yellow woollen sweater, beige twill trousers and a pair of shiny, Italian, brown leather shoes that Douglas would have scorned for himself as being far too light to be practical.

He looked at Douglas, then raised his eyebrows questioningly at Emily, who was standing by grimly, like a watchdog waiting for the order to attack.

'I believe I remember you,' said Alastair.

Doug, at a loss for words, pulled an official card out of his wallet and gave it to Alastair. The card was printed in blue with the coat-of-arms of the Tayside Police; a thistle surrounded by a wreath of its own spiky leaves, surmounted by a crown, with their motto underneath.

'*Semper vigilo*, huh,' said Alastair, reading the motto and ignoring Douglas's name and rank printed in an elegant script below it. 'Does that mean there's only one of you always keeping watch?'

Douglas looked blank; he didn't have the faintest idea what the man was talking about.

'I'm here concerning the death of Moira Dalgleish,' he said.

Alastair smiled, and held out his hand in a curiously formal way. 'Alastair Dalgleish. I'm the brother of Sir Colin, whom I assume you have come to see.' Alastair seemed friendly enough, but his eyes were reserved and watchful.

'I'll be needing to converse with all members of the immediate family of the deceased who are presently residing in this establishment,' said Douglas. His mouth was dry, and he licked his lips.

Alastair seemed entirely unaffected by Douglas's pompous language.

'Thank you, Emily,' he said to the cook, who was still hovering nearby. 'That will be all.'

Emily went back towards the nether regions of the house, and the heavy door closed behind her with a thud.

'Well,' said Alastair, one hand on the big round wooden knob of the banister, 'Let's go up and see Sir Colin. I assume that he's expecting you?'

'He was informed earlier of our impending visitation,' replied Douglas stiffly, blushing with annoyance at not being able to speak plain English in the presence of the gentry.

'He may be asleep, of course,' said Alastair, looking at his watch. 'He sometimes likes to have a wee nap before dinner.'

'Aye, I'd like to be able to do that, too, sometimes,'

Douglas blurted out, and Alastair seemed to be amused by the idea.

Douglas had told Jamieson to meet him at the house and was about to ask if he had appeared, when there was a loud knock at the front door.

'Excuse me,' murmured Alastair, as he went across the bare wooden floor to open the door. Doug watched him; there was something of the athlete about Alastair Dalgleish: his bearing, the way he walked. At the back of his mind he seemed to remember hearing that Alastair had played rugby for Oxford or Cambridge, or some such place. He would have to ask Ian Garvie.

Jamieson was standing on the step. On Alastair's invitation, he came in and for a few moments stood with his head back, gaping up at the dark rafters and high ceiling, which had a barely discernible coat of arms painted in the centre.

'I'm over here, Jamieson,' said Douglas in a loud voice, coming forward. 'Mr Dalgleish, this is Constable Jamieson, who assists me on matters such as this.'

Jamieson's muscular bulk made both Douglas and Alastair look frail, and the stairs creaked under his weight as all three of them walked up with Alastair leading. At the top of the stairs he turned left, and they followed him down a long, musty-odoured corridor. The carpet, a long, faded, rose-coloured oriental runner, had several worn patches, and Jamieson caught his foot in one and almost fell, making the floor shake. Douglas got the impression that there wasn't much money to spend around here, and that so far, Dalgleish House, still impressive from the outside, was threadbare and neglected on the inside.

Sir Colin was in his apartment, which consisted of a large bedroom, a dressing room, and a reception room with a low table, a sofa, and several chairs of different types scattered around. He wasn't asleep, but reclining on the sofa, dressed in an old maroon woollen dressing-gown. He was unshaven, his reddened eyes were wide open, and he wore an expression of sheer misery. Douglas looked at him with a grudging compassion. Usually, his attitude was that if something bad happened to one of the gentry, it made up for the life of luxury and unearned ease they otherwise enjoyed.

Colin sat up. For a moment he seemed dazed and not entirely aware of where he was.

'This is Inspector Niven from the Tayside Police,' said Alastair, ignoring Jamieson's additional presence.

'We're all very sorry about your daughter, sir,' said Douglas gruffly. 'I'm also sorry to have to inform you that there was foul play involved. Miss Moira was murdered, apparently through strangulation.' Doug took a deep breath. 'That means, of course, that there will be an investigation into the matter, of which our presence here is part.'

Doug's statement was followed by a profound silence, broken by Sir Colin. Looking at his brother in a weary, distracted way, he said, 'Does Elspeth know this?'

Alastair looked in turn at Doug, who shook his head.

'Would you ask Lady Elspeth to join us here, please?' Douglas asked Alastair, automatically assuming that he was the one who made decisions and got things done around the house. 'Together with your own wife, sir, if you please.'

Alastair nodded and left.

'Do sit down,' said Colin in a vague, disgruntled way, without looking at either of his visitors. Douglas pointed at a stout wooden chair for Jamieson, then sat himself down in an old purple-covered easy chair facing the sofa. Dust came up from the sides as he lowered himself into it, and a moment later he sneezed.

Sir Colin pulled his dressing-gown around him and fingered his stubbly chin. 'I suppose you'd better tell me now whatever it is I need to know, Inspector.' He was no longer whining, and his voice sounded more assured.

That's only because he's talking to us lowly plebeians, thought Douglas angrily.

'We'll wait until Lady Elspeth and Mr Dalgleish and his wife arrive, sir, if you don't mind,' he said, his voice crisp. Now was the time to show this pathetic creature that the Tayside police force wasn't there just to maintain law and order in the area for the benefit of its hereditary peers. 'I'll want to be speaking to all of you separately, of course, after that.'

The room was chilly, and Doug noticed that a cold draught was coming from under the door. Approaching footsteps were clearly audible; the hollow sounds seemed to resonate in the long, empty corridor. Doug wondered whether it was Lady Elspeth or her sister-in-law Patricia approaching, and why the other one hadn't answered the summons.

It turned out to be Lady Elspeth, dressed in a plain but well-made grey woollen dress, with a red leather belt and high-heeled shoes of the same colour. Unlike Alastair's more exotic footwear from Milan, however, Elspeth's shoes were from Marks & Spencer; good, but nothing fancy.

'Patricia is not available at the moment, I'm afraid,' said Alastair when they came in. He didn't elaborate. Douglas and Jamieson stood up, then, after the introductions, Douglas sat everybody down on chairs where he could see them.

He felt sweaty and uncomfortable at the mere thought of addressing such a group, but he moistened his lips and started. Sir Colin said nothing, but put his head between his hands when Doug repeated that Moira had been strangled. Tears slid between his fingers and rolled down the backs of his hands.

From time to time Elspeth looked over at Colin with a tenderness mixed with distress, but mostly she watched Douglas's face. 'Do you have any idea who might have done this?' she asked.

'All I wanted to do was inform you of the post-mortem findings,' replied Douglas. 'And now I'd like to speak to each one of you separately.' His eyes went from Elspeth to Alastair, then over to Colin, who was still soundlessly weeping, then they went back, speculative, polite, but with predatory expression to Lady Elspeth. 'Starting with you, m'lady, if you don't mind.'

Chapter Eight

During the day, Rory McDermott worked as a fork-lift truck operator at the Tayside bonded whisky warehouse on the outskirts of town. His job involved unloading and stacking cases of bottled whisky from the distillers and transporting them from the racks in the bonded part of the warehouse to the loading bay. There his load was checked first by a company employee then by a government inspector before being loaded on to the trucks. The job was not particularly demanding, but today Rory had been reprimanded twice for inattention. The first time he had backed his fork-lift into a tall stack of empty cardboard boxes; no major damage had been done but several dozen boxes were ruined and the foreman happened to be standing right next to them. The second time, he had come round a corner too fast and almost collided with a group of visiting Japanese businessmen.

'One more time and you're out, Rory,' he was told by the irritated foreman, who had helped to pick up and dust off a small Japanese gentleman who had tripped and landed flat on his back on the concrete floor while jumping out of the truck's way. Luckily for Rory, his work record up to that time was good. Pulling himself together, he tried to ignore the paralysing feeling in his stomach, and managed to finish the interminable day

without any further incident. But Dan McKerron, the
foreman, had certainly looked at him strangely, as if he
could see that something weird was going on with him.

Rory parked his vehicle in the corner of the
warehouse, and walked out past the security guards to
the employees' car-park, his mind full of so many
frightening things that he couldn't think straight.

Bella was already home making dinner when he
pulled up outside the house.

'Miss Moira's a' they're talking about,' she told him
without looking up from the potatoes she was peeling in
the sink. Bella worked for an office-cleaning company
in Perth, and her fellow-workers were an inexhaustible
source of gossip, some of it reliable, some less so. 'One
of them said her husband came back from the grave and
killed her out of revenge.'

Rory, who had an obsession about cleanliness, went
straight to the bathroom next to the kitchen, and took
off his clothes. Through the open door she could see
him, pale, wiry, and obviously uncomfortable about
what she had just said.

With one hand on the plastic shower curtain, he
replied, 'That's just a load of nonsense.'

There was a long, heavy silence, then Bella turned
away abruptly. 'Well, you should know,' she said.

Sir Colin was obviously not pleased to have the
interviews conducted in his study, but according to
Alastair, it was the only suitable place in the house.
Douglas suspected that it might be the only heated room
besides the kitchen and the bedrooms.

Sir Colin wrapped a blanket around himself and,
looking vaguely confused and childishly resentful,
refused to move.

Lady Elspeth sat down on the edge of Colin's sofa
and gripped her knees, watching Doug with a scared,
bird-like expression, her eyes going over to Colin every
so often, as if the added responsibility she bore for him

was simply too much for her to deal with.

'We'll move along as fast as we can, ma'am,' said Doug stolidly, wondering how he would feel if his daughter had been strangled and then dumped in the river. Elspeth seemed numbed by her bereavement.

'First,' he went on, 'I understand that Miss Moira's husband is dead?'

'Yes, he is,' replied Elspeth. 'He got typhoid soon after going to Hong Kong. He died there. The poor man never even saw his baby.'

'Oh, I'm sorry,' said Douglas, uselessly. 'Are there relatives? Of the husband, I mean?'

'I don't believe so,' replied Elspeth hesitantly. 'Aside from an aunt who lived near Canterbury and brought him up. If there were other relatives, Moira never mentioned them.'

'Can you tell me when you last saw Miss Moira?' Douglas asked gently. Elspeth was as tense as a piano wire, and in spite of himself he felt sorry for her. It seemed that she had had a lot to put up with in addition to her grief over Moira's death.

'It was just a week ago, Inspector, the day before we reported her missing.'

'Did she give any indication that she might be in danger? Had she mentioned anyone that she might have been afraid of?'

'I don't think she was afraid of anyone, as far as I know. She was strong and healthy . . .' Her voice shook. 'Of course, she might not have told me because she didn't talk to me much about her personal affairs.'

'Do you know of anyone who might have had a grudge of some sort against her?'

Elspeth hesitated. 'She's had quite a number of men friends,' she said, choosing her words carefully. 'And some of them, well, they didn't always want to go away when she wanted them to go away.'

'What men friends?' asked Douglas, looking over at Jamieson to make sure he was taking notes. 'Who

specifically are the persons you are referring to?' His
Glaswegian accent seemed more pronounced.

'Well, since Moira came back from Hong Kong . . .'
Elspeth paused, trying to find the briefest way of
explaining herself, '. . . with the baby . . .' As if in
answer to her words, they heard a child crying, not too
far away. 'That's him,' she went on anxiously, looking
over at Colin again. He was staring straight ahead,
apparently unaware of the others in the room.
'Anyway, Moira developed a number of friendships,
but none of them lasted very long, to my knowledge.'

'Names?' Douglas looked again at Jamieson, who
dutifully poised his ballpoint pen over his open
notebook.

'Well, there was a young schoolteacher in Perth. I
don't even remember his name.' She glanced at Colin as
if for help, then shrugged despondently. 'I do know he
emigrated to Canada several months ago.'

'Anyone else?' asked Douglas persistently.

A faint flush appeared on Elspeth's face. 'This is
really rather embarrassing,' she said, her grey eyes
refusing to meet Douglas's. 'Moira didn't have the best
taste in men, I'm afraid.'

Douglas tightened his lips. It was becoming obvious
to him that underneath her nervousness, Elspeth wasn't
any different from the rest of these aristocrats.

'It seems that Moira had a rather tempestuous
relationship with a young man who worked on the
estate,' went on Elspeth.

'Name?'

Jamieson looked up expectantly.

Elspeth put a shaky hand up to her forehead. 'I don't
remember . . . Roy, I think it was, or something like
that. Ask Alastair, I'm sure he'd remember.'

'Was the man's name Rory, by any chance, ma'am?'
asked Jamieson, unexpectedly. Elspeth turned to him as
if she hadn't noticed his presence, although Jamieson's
size made that unlikely.

'That's right,' she said. 'Rory McDermott. He was the ghillie. I tried to talk to Moira about him, to warn her, but she wouldn't listen.'

'Warn her?' asked Douglas quickly. 'Warn her about what?'

'That he was really not a suitable person for her.' Elspeth was wringing her hands in her distress. 'The man was already married, or at least had a woman living with him.'

'When did all this take place, Lady Elspeth?'

'Oh, just a few weeks after she came back from Hong Kong. We were all terribly shocked.'

'So what happened?'

'Well, Alastair was furious with her,' replied Elspeth, looking at the floor. 'Rory lived in one of the estate cottages, and was coming up to the house all the time, although he was warned not to. So Alastair had to get rid of him, obviously.'

Like an insect that happened to annoy him, thought Doug, smouldering. Not that he had any feeling for Rory McDermott; the man was obviously a fool to mess around with someone like Moira Dalgleish. What bothered him was the callous way in which these blue-bloods dealt with ordinary working people.

'Anybody else?' asked Doug.

Elspeth sighed. 'Probably,' she answered. 'I don't know. She always had a mind of her own and never listened to what anybody told her.'

'Did she at least heed her father?' asked Doug, sounding stern, and thinking how *he* was going to raise his son or daughter.

Elspeth looked helplessly over at Colin. 'She didn't heed anyone, except maybe Alastair, on occasion, but he was about the only one with any kind of influence over her.'

'What did Miss Moira do with her time?' asked Douglas, ponderous again. 'Was she gainfully employed at the time of her demise?'

Elspeth looked dully at him. 'Do you mean did she have a job? Well, she had something to do with a hairdresser's salon and went there a couple of afternoons a week. Perhaps she had some kind of financial interest in it. Maybe Colin . . .' Again she looked over at her husband, who now had curled up in a foetal position at the other end of the long couch. 'I don't know what she did there. I don't suppose she actually did perms and things herself.'

'Name of the establishment?'

' "*Salon de Beauté*",' said Elspeth. 'It's on South Street. The man who runs it is called Armand Thierry.'

Jamieson's pencil paused in mid-air, and he threw Douglas a silent cry for help.

'Would you spell that, please?' Douglas asked Elspeth on Jamieson's behalf. 'The name of the shop and the foreign man's name.'

Elspeth did so.

'Lady Dalgleish,' said Douglas, sitting back, 'can you think of anything else that might help us find the person who killed your daughter?'

Elspeth shook her head slowly, and tears were brimming in her eyes.

'Thank you, ma'am,' said Douglas gently, 'That'll be all. We'd like to take a look at Moira's room, if you don't mind,' he went on. 'After we've talked to the others.'

'Of course,' Elspeth got up, and Colin, apparently startled by her movement, sat bolt upright and looked around him. His wife gently took him by the arm and led him into the adjacent bedroom before departing through the study.

Douglas and Jamieson watched her leave the room.

'She's scared,' said Jamieson, pointing towards the door after it closed. 'She's sad, but she's scared, too.'

'Just go and tell Mr Alastair we'll be back to talk to him tomorrow morning, Jamieson,' said Douglas sharply, looking at his watch. Jamieson seemed offended, so Doug added in a milder tone, 'As for her, you never can tell with that kind of upper-class person, lad.' He shook his head. 'The likes of them, women and men too, you never know what they're really feeling. Their blood's a' thinned, and any real sentiment they ever had is long-since washed out. So they have to put on an act.'

'Nae like us,' replied Jamieson, rejoicing in the newly appreciated richness of his own genetic pool. He stood up, slipped the elastic band around his notebook and went to find Alastair.

Douglas stopped in for a chat with Jean on his way home. She was in the kitchen, preparing dinner, feeling tired and a bit grumpy, but she remembered to give him Moira's address book. He flipped through it. 'Did you look at this?' he asked after a few moments.

'No,' replied Jean, 'and the only reason you're seeing it is because she was murdered.'

'Do you know anybody called A. Larkin?'

'Arnie Larkin,' said Jean, busy peeling potatoes. 'He's at the *Courier*. Why?

'Moira had an appointment to see him a couple of days ago,' replied Doug, sombrely. He flipped through the rest of the book. On the last two facing pages were columns of numbers; one page was headed A, the other RSVP. Doug stared at them for a moment. 'What do you make of this?' he asked, holding the book open in front of her at the sink.

'I've no idea,' replied Jean, raising her eyes to the pages for a moment. 'You're the detective, not me.' Doug put the book in his pocket, intending to examine it further at some later time.

'Do you want to stay for dinner?' asked Jean, knowing that he would want to go home to Cathie; Doug often needed a small stimulus of that sort, to make him leave.

* * *

Back at home, Doug looked in the phone book for Arnie Larkin, and dialled his number.

Arnie sounded like a cheerful young man. 'Yes,' he said, when Doug asked him about his scheduled meeting with Moira, 'we were going to have coffee at the theatre restaurant. It's so sad about her . . .'

'Business or pleasure?' asked Doug.

There was a brief silence, then Arnie laughed. 'Business, I assure you. About a year ago, there was a rumour that she was going off to get married, so I phoned her for an interview, because, you know, the Dalgleishes are always news around here, and I wanted to know more about her husband-to-be.'

'Did you get it?'

'No. She was actually a bit snooty, which is unlike her. Anyway, she came in to the office a couple of weeks ago, rather tense, I thought. She came with her baby and said she was ready to talk about his father. I knew by then that Mr Glashan had died in Hong Kong or somewhere like that, but I was on my way out on a job with a photographer so I couldn't interview her then. So we set it up for last Tuesday.'

Doug was about to ask some more questions, but Cathie called saying that dinner was on the table, and he knew better than to keep her waiting. 'I'll get back to you if anything else turns up,' he said quickly. 'Thanks for your help.'

Chapter Nine

For the entire previous day, Armand Thierry had stayed at home, drawn the curtains in every room, lain on his bed and wept. Or so he told the four respectfully assembled women he employed when, the day after Moira's body was found, he reopened his small but exclusive beauty salon on South Street.

'It's been a quite, quite unbearable personal loss for me, my dears,' he told them, but his eyes were dry, and he glanced at the delicate Meissen clock set in front of the high mirrors. It was two minutes before opening time, and nobody had any doubt that the doors would open on the dot, as usual. 'We'll work hard, desperately hard, as a tribute to her, won't we, ladies? Now let's . . .'

His expression froze, and the women turned to see what had stopped him in mid-sentence. Outside, tapping on the small glass window, was Elspeth Dalgleish.

'Well, don't just stand there, Doris,' he snapped at the young woman nearest the door. 'Let the lady in!'

Lady Elspeth entered, obviously trying not to look scared, glanced quickly at the women who were staring at her, and came up to Armand. 'Do you have a moment, please, Mr Thierry? I'd like to speak to you in private.'

He turned without a word and she followed him into
the tiny office at the back of the shop. Elspeth seemed
even more nervous now that she was alone with him,
and wouldn't sit down when he offered her a chair. She
stood near the door, looking ready to run.

'Mr Thierry,' she said, licking her dry lips, 'my
daughter left a folder with a great deal of information
about you. I don't want it, I don't want to know
anything about you. I . . . I just want to sell you that
folder.' Her voice was almost inaudible. 'You see, I
know the reason you were making payments to her.'

Armand's mouth opened, but no sound came out.
His face seemed to change and he stared at Elspeth with
an expression which made her insides turn over, but she
held her ground. She needed money, and there was no
other way she could think of to get it.

'Blackmail is a criminal offence,' said Armand,
speaking very quietly. 'I could simply tell the police and
have you put away for a very long time.'

'I'm not blackmailing you,' replied Elspeth, seeming
to gain a little courage. 'I'm just offering you something
you want and I don't want.' For the first time since she
had arrived, Elspeth raised her eyes to meet his. 'In any
case, you know what would happen if you went to the
police, Mr Thierry. You'd be the loser.'

'Assuming that I was in the market for that folder,'
said Armand slowly, 'how much would it cost me? And
how would I know that you didn't have copies made?'

Elspeth looked offended, like a mouse being accused
of armed robbery. 'Of course I wouldn't keep copies,'
she said. 'For one thing it would be terribly dishonest,
and in any case I never want to hear about you or *it* ever
again.'

'How much?' Armand's fingers were opening and
closing and whether he did it for effect or not, Elspeth
noticed. In spite of her fear she managed to tell him the
figure she had decided on.

Armand whistled through clenched teeth. 'It would

take me several weeks to collect such an amount,' he said, staring at Elspeth as if he were measuring the distance between them.

'Two weeks,' said Elspeth through dry lips.

'And if I can't raise that huge amount?' asked Armand.

Elspeth shrugged her little shoulders. 'Then the folder goes to Inspector Niven,' she said.

On the way out, Elspeth saw Jean Montrose coming in for her weekly wash and blow-dry. Elspeth was surprised, but she recovered quickly. 'I'll see you on Sunday, Dr Montrose,' she said, but didn't stop. Jean nodded, but out of the corner of her eye, she saw Armand coming out of the office Elspeth had left, and to her astonishment, there was something quite frightening about his normally affable expression. When he saw Jean, his expression changed, and she thought it might have been a trick of the light, and as he came over he was so charming and attentive that she soon put her momentary misgivings out of her mind.

Douglas was having a slight problem with the Dalgleish men. Colin refused to say anything unless Alastair was present in the room with him, and finally Douglas relented. At the back of his mind was Bob McLeod's admonition to watch his step because of the high-level attention the case was getting.

They all sat down; Colin with a petulant pout on his face, and Alastair with the same tolerant expression he had before. He was obviously well used to his older brother's ineffectiveness, and was doing his best to help him get through this tiresome interview with the detectives.

Douglas asked the same questions, more or less, that he'd asked Elspeth. The last time Colin had seen his daughter was at dinner the day before she disappeared. She'd seemed perfectly normal, he thought.

'Actually, Colin, you had dinner in your rooms that evening,' murmured Alastair. 'Don't you remember?

Patricia and I had just come back from London.'
Alastair shot a slightly apologetic look at Doug. 'And
you didn't want to see anyone.'

Colin jumped up, and Jamieson, startled,
accidentally jammed the point of his pen into the back
of his hand. Colin faced Douglas, his lips quivering, and
stuck out his wrists, holding them together. 'All right
then,' he said to Doug in a hysterical tone, 'why don't
you arrest me? On the testimony of my brother,' he
flashed a look at Alastair, 'I've obviously been trying to
mislead you.' To everyone's embarrassment, tears
formed in Colin's eyes, and started to roll down his
cheeks.

'Please sit down, Sir Colin,' said Doug, gruffly,
looking at the floor. 'We know this is a difficult time for
you. All I'm trying to find out is the movements of Miss
Moira before . . .'

'Before some swine came here and strangled her!'
shouted Colin. He started to pace up and down, shaking
off Alastair's gentle attempts to restrain him. The tears
were flowing freely now, and the sound of his
unrestrained sobbing was utterly unnerving to both
Douglas and Jamieson.

'Maybe we should finish this some other time,'
muttered Douglas to Alastair. 'I dinna think his
recollection is at its very best right now.'

'Good idea, Inspector,' replied Alastair, looking at
his brother. 'I think I can probably tell you what you
need to know.'

Colin collapsed back on the sofa and lay down on it,
curling his legs and burying his face in his hands, while
Alastair slid along the sofa to make room for him.

'Moira and Elspeth were just finishing dinner when
my wife and I arrived.' Alastair hesitated. 'I think they
had been having a . . . well . . . a heated discussion.'

'A fight?' asked Jamieson, looking up. This was
sounding more like home territory now.

'No, certainly not,' replied Alastair, annoyed. 'We don't fight in this family.'

'I'm sorry, Mr Dalgleish,' said Doug, throwing a warning glance at Jamieson. 'Please go on.'

'The baby was in a crib near the table. He was crying, and Moira went over and picked him up . . .' He paused again. 'Snatched him up might be more accurate. Then she left the room, saying she'd see us in the morning.'

'Were you personally on good terms with Miss Moira, sir?' asked Doug.

'Patricia and me? Oh, yes, certainly. I suppose she was my favourite niece. We don't have children of our own, and we'd go hiking with her, things like that. A bit headstrong, Moira, perhaps, but there's nothing wrong with that.' Alastair smiled. 'She was a very clever judge of people. She always found what made them tick. I suppose I spoiled her . . .' Alastair glanced at Colin, who was taking no part in the proceedings and seemed to have gone to sleep. 'There isn't much money here as I'm sure you're aware, and I did try to make life a little more comfortable for her.'

'Did you see Miss Moira after that brief encounter?' asked Doug.

Alastair shook his head. 'Next morning, early, Elspeth heard the baby crying, and he wouldn't stop, so she went to see what was happening. He was hungry, poor little chap, and Moira was nowhere to be found.'

'Do you know if her bed had been slept in? Was there any sign of a struggle?'

'I really wouldn't know,' replied Alastair. He rubbed the side of his head with the heel of his hand. 'Elspeth could tell you, I suppose. Anyway, she came to tell me about Moira. She was really put out, I mean Elspeth was. We couldn't imagine that she'd just leave the baby like that, because Moira had always been devoted to Denys and took very good care of him.'

'Had she ever done anything like that before? Just taken off without telling anybody?' Douglas asked, trying not to sound too disapproving.

Alastair hesitated for a moment. 'Well, I don't know because we don't live here, but I believe that when she went off, for any reason, she always made sure that the baby was being taken care of.'

'She'd go off once or twice a week,' said Colin, sitting up suddenly. 'Maybe not as often since the baby was born. Sometimes she didn't come back until the next day.'

Colin then lay down again, curled his legs up and closed his eyes.

'Is there a nanny who takes care of him?'

Alastair shook his head. 'Emily usually took care of the baby. He's pretty good and isn't any trouble. You met Emily in the kitchen when you came in, didn't you?'

'Doesn't Lady Elspeth ever look after him?'

Jamieson, who was having difficulty keeping up with the conversation, sighed loudly and tried to write faster.

'She's scared of babies,' said Colin from his horizontal position on the couch. His eyes were still tightly closed. 'Especially this one, I think.'

Doug raised his eyebrows and looked at Alastair, whe gave a barely perceptible shrug of the shoulders.

It didn't seem to Doug that there was much more to be gained here. 'Is there any more pertinent information you would care to divulge to us?' he asked Alastair. Doug was still powerless to use everyday words with the Dalgleishes, although he didn't feel threatened by Alastair, and certainly poor Colin didn't seem enough to set off Doug's socially triggered logopathy.

'I don't think so,' replied Alastair.

Doug looked at Jamieson and nodded. Sometimes Jamieson's artless questions set off a useful train of investigation, usually because the interviewees often didn't bother to think very hard about his question and could leave themselves open for a more penetrating follow-up from Doug.

But Jamieson had nothing to ask. He snapped the elastic band round his notebook, loudly enough to indicate that he'd done enough writing for this morning, thank you very much.

'Would it be permissible for us to take a look at Miss Moira's room?' asked Doug, standing up.

Alastair hesitated for only a second. 'Yes, I suppose that's all right. Elspeth would . . . Yes, of course, if you'll please follow me.'

Alastair pulled the door open and almost ran into a tall, severely dressed, haughty-looking woman with big grey eyes, blonde hair of dubious origin and a chilly expression. Doug remembered her sitting in the back seat of the Jaguar on the morning Moira's body was found. To Doug's sensitive mind, her eyes looked like scanners that would first determine the precise social class of anyone within a micro-second, then dismiss them if they came below hers.

'Patricia!' Alastair looked flustered and annoyed by her sudden appearance. He turned back to Doug and Jamieson, who had almost run into him. 'Patricia, these gentlemen are from the police. They're investigating Moira's death.'

'Good morning, ma'am,' muttered Douglas, quite over awed by the woman who stood in the doorway staring at him with such cold disdain. He touched his forehead in an awkward salute.

'We were about to go to Moira's room, dear,' said Alastair. 'Would you care to join us?'

Douglas, disgusted with what he interpreted as an artificial tone in their conversation, wanted to say 'and do bring your own racquet', or some equally trenchant comment, but instead murmured, 'We'd like to speak with you afterwards, ma'am, if that would be convenient.'

Patricia nodded, looking straight through him. Doug

felt slight consolation when he noted that she wasn't any more amiable with her husband.

Douglas and Jamieson followed them down another long, bleak corridor. Their footsteps rang on the uncarpeted, wooden floor, and Douglas noticed that the wall had light-coloured oblong patches along it where paintings had hung. The corridor had originally been lit by small silver-and-crystal chandeliers every dozen feet or so, but most of them were missing, and had been replaced either with nothing or by bare, forty-watt bulbs hanging down by a length of flex from the high, dark ceiling. They must have sold the paintings and the fixtures, thought Douglas, and wondered what would happen when they were all gone. There didn't seem to be much left now.

Alastair stopped in front of a closed door near the end of the corridor, opened it and allowed Douglas and Jamieson to go in first. Doug stood just inside the door, and put one cautionary hand on Jamieson's arm to prevent him from going further. 'Just look first,' he said. 'First impressions are sometimes important.'

'How long do you think you'll be?' asked Alastair.

'Half an hour, maybe,' replied Doug.

'We'll come back, then,' Alastair looked at his watch, 'in thirty minutes.'

After the door closed, Jamieson muttered, 'This place and these people give me the creeps, sir.'

'Just pay attention to what you're supposed to be doing, Jamieson,' snapped Doug, who, too, was feeling a kind of mild apprehension. 'You sound like a girl guide on her first night hike.'

Jamieson flushed. Every time he tried to show his sensitivity and his feeling for atmosphere, the inspector shot him down in flames. 'Fingerprint precautions, sir?' he asked stiffly.

Doug hesitated for a second. The room was untidy, but there was no sign of a struggle. Of course, it was quite possible that Moira had willingly accompanied the killer out of the chamber.

'Yes, I suppose so,' he replied. 'You'd better go and call in the forensic boys. They can sweep for hair and fibres as well as check for prints, although I'll bet there won't be any except her own.'

Jamieson went off, and Douglas stood there, thinking, trying without a great deal of success to put himself in the shoes of an aristocratic young widow with a small child and a reputedly sharp eye for the men.

The low bed was made, neatly enough. A thick extra blanket was folded over the foot. So unless someone had come in later to make it, Moira hadn't slept in her bed that night. An unopened blue box of disposable nappies lay on the floor by the bed next to a brightly coloured yellow and blue rattle. A set of almost new silver hairbrushes and a hair-dryer, still plugged into the wall socket, were on the dresser. An oversized silver-framed photograph on the bedside table caught Doug's eye and he stepped forward to look at it. The black-and-white portrait was of a very handsome, smiling young man, presumably Moira's husband. Scribbled across the bottom in large letters were the words *To Moira, with all my love*, but the signature was illegible.

The wardrobe was half-open and half-full of clothes, hanging tidily. Doug noticed that the skirts hung on short wooden hangers similar to the ones Cathie used. Shoes of different colours and styles were arranged in a neat row below the clothes. Doug took out his handkerchief and used it to open the dresser drawers without leaving prints on the handles. The top drawer contained knick-knacks, a small silver pocket knife with Moira's initials, lots of gold-coloured tubes of makeup, mascara, jars of various kinds of what he assumed was face-cream. Looking rather helplessly at all this female paraphernalia, Douglas wished that Jean had come with him as some kind of translator. The middle drawers contained sweaters, shorts that he noticed were *very* short, and the bottom two contained underwear. There was a lot of it, silky, very insubstantial stuff. Douglas fumbled gingerly through it. Some of it was black and lacy, with holes in unexpected places. It was not at all the kind of thing he was used to seeing at home, and he rather hastily concluded that there was really nothing here that could help him in any way.

He was relieved to find Moira's handbag in the adjoining sitting room; in his experience, a woman's handbag was often the best source of information about its owner.

It was a simple black calf-skin bag with a gold clasp. Again using his handkerchief, Douglas opened it. Even after all those years, he still felt a twinge of deep-seated guilt when peering inside a woman's handbag. Then he upended the bag on to the coffee table, and everything spilled out, loose change, car keys, a handkerchief, and more makeup. He pounced on a blue chequebook.

The door opened and Jamieson came back in. 'The forensics 'll be here in half an hour,' he said.

'Good,' said Doug. He picked up the chequebook and started to flip through the pages. There were the usual records of deposits and cheques written, but nothing that stood out as unusual. 'I'm removing this,' he said. 'Do you have a bag and a form?'

Jamieson reached out in his pocket for a plastic evidence bag with its attached form, which Douglas filled out and Jamieson signed as a witness.

'Did you find anything, sir?' asked Jamieson, looking around the room.

'Nothing of any use to us, I don't think.' Doug's mind went back to Rory McDermott, and he looked at his watch. Alastair Dalgleish would be back any minute now, Douglas sighed. It was late, he was tired, and he decided to wait until next morning before going to look for McDermott.

'We'll leave the door open for the forensic lads,'

Doug said, 'then you can lock up after we've talked to Patricia.' Using her Christian name gave Doug a strange but short-lived feeling of equality.

'I'm going to be late for my supper,' said Jamieson, aggrieved. 'My mother—'

'Phone her,' interrupted Douglas impatiently. 'Tell her you're on a mission of vital importance and won't be home till nine.'

Alastair came back to escort them to Colin's study, where Patricia was waiting for them, elegant legs crossed nonchalantly. She wasn't able to tell them much more about Moira than Alastair already had.

'She had what looked to me like very expensive clothes hanging up in her room,' said Douglas. 'Very expensive shoes, too, I would say.'

Patricia stared at him. 'Is that a question?'

Douglas sighed. 'Well, yes. Her mother and father obviously have difficulty making ends meet, and so all these designer outfits seemed, I don't know, out of place, if you see what I mean.'

'She had other sources of income, I suppose,' said Patricia, flicking her hand dismissively. 'I imagine she had a few rich boyfriends whe would have bought clothes and things for her.'

'Do you know of any such rich boyfriends, Mrs Dalgleish, or is that just a supposition on your part?'

'It's never crossed my mind,' said Patricia haughtily, 'I never paid attention to what Moira wore.'

Doug looked coolly at her, feeling a sense of comfort when he found one of them lying so obviously. Even to Jamieson the idea that Patricia, who dressed well and carefully, should not notice what her niece wore, sounded unlikely.

'Do you know if Moira had any outside income?' asked Douglas.

An idea struck Patricia, and Douglas could almost hear the thump. It was becoming clear that Patricia Dalgleish, for all her sophisticated airs, was not very bright. 'I think Moira got money from a life insurance policy when her husband died,' she said. 'In fact, I'm sure she did. That's how she had money to spend.'

According to Patricia, Moira had been high-spirited, had a mind of her own, was fond of the baby, and liked to have a good time. Towards the end of the interview, Patricia said, referring to Moira, 'There was really something irresistible about that girl.' There was more than a hint of malice mixed with jealously in her face, and it didn't add to Patricia's charm. 'When she wanted a man, that was it. They never got away. Never.'

'Whew,' said Jamieson after Patricia had gone. He closed his notebook with a subdued snap. 'She's scary.'

Douglas was just happy the interview was over. His opinions about people tended to simmer and take shape hours or even days after talking with them, so he merely growled at Jamieson about the risks of making hasty judgements, and offered no comment of his own.

Chapter Ten

It was getting dark and very cold when Jean left the surgery, and she had trouble starting her car. She was just about to give up and call Steven to come and rescue her when the motor caught and off she went.

Suncrest Nursing Home was on Barossa Place, and Jean had no difficulty finding a parking space nearby. The snow had been cleared from the ramp, and Jean walked in. The matron's friendly, old, honey-coloured spaniel came and sniffed at her, but Jean was too preoccupied to do more than pat the arthritic dog on the head. Mrs Kimball was in her office, and stood up when Jean came in. That was always a bad sign. Mrs Kimball was a large, competent woman with a countrywoman's ruddy cheeks and uncompromising streaks of iron-grey in her hair, tucked up inside an old-fashioned nurse's cap.

'Thank you for coming, Dr Montrose,' she said, in a formal tone. That was another bad sign; like many other people, Mrs Kimball usually called her 'Dr Jean'.

'I suppose it was our fault,' she went on, 'but here at Suncrest, we're not used to having to search patients' rooms for . . . well, for contraband.' Mrs Kimball seemed to swell up at the mere thought of using such prison-like tactics, and Jean watched her, in fascination: the matron always wore her uniform a couple of sizes too small for her ample figure, and now Jean felt certain that she was going to witness a whole row of buttons fly off from this excessive tension. The material stretched, the buttonholes quivered, but every button did its duty and the emergency subsided.

'Tell me what happened, Mrs Kimball?' Jean asked. 'Do you mind if I sit down? I've had a long day.'

'Of course.' The matron subsided into her own chair. She found it difficult to be angry with the 'wee doc', particularly when the problem obviously wasn't her fault.

'Well . . .' Mrs Kimball adjusted herself in the chair, and a different set of buttons took up the strain. 'Everything seemed all right this morning, and Mrs Findlay ate her dinner just fine . . .' She paused, and folded her arms, which fitted comfortably on the horizontal shelf made by her bosom. 'Mrs Findlay usually has a reason for doing things,' she said, thoughtfully. 'Like the time she started the fire, or when she walked naked into the Board of Governors' meeting.'

Jean was about to protest that her mother had never walked naked into any board meeting, but it was clear that her mother's escapades had been magnified by numerous retellings, and had now entered the local folklore in their final form. So Jean made a faint placatory noise but, otherwise, said nothing.

'The only reason I can think of,' went on Mrs Kimball, 'is that we did have fish fingers for lunch, and it was the third time this week, but our cook was off, and the only thing the girl Maureen knows how to prepare is fish fingers . . .'

Jean stood up. 'I'd better go and see her,' she said. 'Is she all right now?'

'Yes. She's back in bed.' Mrs Kimball hesitated. 'Dr Montrose, do you happen to know a ballad that starts ''Aye Aye, Cathusalem''?'

'I think I've heard it,' said Jean. 'A bit bawdy, isn't it?'

'Bawdy scarcely describes it, Dr Montrose. As far as I could tell, it's about the adventures of a harlot in Jerusalem . . .'

'That's what makes the rhyme,' said Jean, almost to herself.

'I beg your pardon?'

'Cathusalem and Jerusalem. It doesn't matter.'

'Well, your mother was singing it this afternoon, out in the corridor, at the top of her voice with a bottle of sherry in her hand,' said Mrs Kimball grimly. 'During visiting hours. She refused to stop or go back into her room. I don't need to tell you that it caused a major disturbance.'

'Oh dear,' said Jean. 'I'm surprised she knows the words.'

When Jean walked down the corridor a few moments later and went into her mother's darkened room, Mrs Findlay was wide awake in bed and spoke in her usual authoritative tone. 'Do *not* turn on the lights, Jean, and do *not* speak above a whisper. I have a severe headache, and urgently need medication to relieve the pain, but the imbecile attendants here have refused point-blank to minister to my needs.'

Jean sat down on the comfortable chintz-covered chair near the window.

'What happened, Mother?'

'What happened? I just wanted to liven things up a bit around here. It's like living in a cemetery. Everybody creeps around, talking in whispers, and then they feed us poisoned fish fingers to knock off all the dying old crones littered around this place.'

'So you went out and sang "Cathusalem" in the corridor?'

'I did remember to take my Zimmer,' said Mrs Findlay, who had suffered a complicated fracture of the hip some months before, and was in the nursing home for recuperation.

'Thank goodness,' said Jean, smiling. 'But Mother, why did you have to get drunk?'

'Don't be ridiculous,' snapped Mrs Findlay. 'Of course I wasn't drunk. You just have to be careful in a place like this.'

Jean waited for an explanation, but her mother needed the stimulus of a question to keep going. She'd always been like that, Jean remembered. It was her way of getting the undivided attention of her audience, and it also gave her the false notion that she wasn't monopolizing the conversation.

'Why do you have to be careful in a place like this, Mother?'

Mrs Findlay moved in her bed. 'Jean, I don't know why you insist on sitting in the dark like this,' she said in an irritated voice. 'Please turn the light on so that I can see you.'

Jean went to the door and flipped the light switch, while her mother kept talking. 'Well, because if I had just got up and started singing that kind of song, they'd have assumed I had lost my marbles, they would have summoned a psychiatrist and I'd have been packed off to the nearest loony bin. So I pretended to drink a bottle of sherry. By the way, I prefer Harvey's Bristol Cream, although I know it's more expensive than the stuff you usually bring.'

Mrs Findlay fixed her daughter with a distinctly bleary eye. 'You have to understand, Jean, in a place like this, it's *not* OK to be insane, but it *is* OK to be drunk. And let me tell you, when I got going, I did liven the place up.' Mrs Findlay grinned, totally unrepentant. 'I could hear a couple of the old biddies across the hall. They loved it. They even joined in the chorus.'

Jean shook her head, trying not to laugh.

Mrs Findlay moaned suddenly and put her hands to

her head. 'Could I at least have some aspirin for my headache? Or have you joined the conspiracy with the staff here?'

Jean took a small sample container from her purse and broke the foil. She got up, went to the sink, found a glass and put some water in it.

'Here, Mother. Two pills. Here's some water to wash them down.'

Mrs Findlay took the pills in one hand and Jean placed the glass in the other.

Her mother looked at the pale yellow pills. 'Those aren't aspirins,' she said sharply. 'What are you trying to do to me?'

'They're a new kind of headache pill,' replied Jean patiently. 'If you take them we won't need to bother the nurses, who have other things to do.'

Mrs Findlay deliberately dropped the pills on the floor. 'I'd be found dead in bed tomorrow morning, no doubt,' she said. 'Natural causes, that's what they'd call it at the inquest, for certain. Thanks anyway.'

Jean shrugged, and felt her patience ebbing, but she went to get a couple of aspirins from Mrs Kimball. When she got back, her mother was asleep, and Jean crept out, feeling a sense of relief mixed with guilt as she gently closed the door behind her.

On the way home, Jean stopped at Marks & Spencer for some haddock and a bag of frozen prawns for dinner.

Nobody was in when she got home, and she felt a small, guilty feeling of relief at the prospect of having a few minutes all to herself. She put her cardboard box of NHS forms in the sitting room, expecting to spend her usual couple of hours after dinner writing letters to consultants, and doing some of the tedious paperwork that nowadays was an inevitable addendum to every medical move she made, every prescription she wrote.

There was a small pile of letters on the hall table, and

a laboriously written note from Mrs Cattanach, the cleaning lady, saying that she needed more ammonia and furniture polish.

Fiona and Lisbie came home almost at the same time, and they helped Jean prepare dinner so that it was ready by the time Steven returned from work.

'Anything new on the Dalgleish business?' enquired Steven when they had all sat down.

'She was strangled,' Jean replied quickly, hoping that the subject would now be closed. 'Do you want butter on your peas, dear?'

'Strangled?' said Lisbie. She shuddered. 'How horrible.'

'I thought Moira drowned,' said Fiona, passing the plate up to her father. 'Isn't that what you told us yesterday?'

'I didn't know then,' replied Jean. 'Let's talk about something else, if you don't mind. What happened at work today?'

'Nothing much. Mum, do they know who did it?'

'Fiona, would you pass the salt and pepper up to your father, please?'

'They're right in front of him, Mum.' Fiona had the fixed notion that life in the Montrose household was arranged solely to maximize Steven's comfort, and she resented this.

'I can reach them, thanks,' said Steven, throwing a cold glance at Fiona, and for a moment Jean thought that the conversation had effectively been sidetracked. But not for long; this time Steven, who usually knew better, was the culprit. 'Somebody at work said Moira Dalgleish got married just to have a baby.'

'For heaven's sake, Dad,' said Fiona, irritated. 'Wake up. Women don't do that nowadays. If they want a baby, they just go ahead and have one, right, Lisbie?'

'That's what you're going to do, isn't it, Fiona?' Lisbie's big eyes rested, admiringly for once, on her sister. Fiona had so much self-confidence she could get away with something like that and be happy, whereas Lisbie knew she had neither the nerve nor the resources to have a baby without first getting married.

'*Is* that what you propose to do, Fiona?' Steven asked, his face turning red. 'Because if it is—'

'It would save the price of a big wedding and reception,' said Jean, smiling to restore calm.

'That's *not* the point,' said Steven, putting down his fork with a clang. His voice rose. 'I don't mind paying whatever is necessary—'

'To get rid of Fiona, heh, heh,' interjected Lisbie under her breath, grinning at her sister. 'I'd go along with that.'

'Please, everybody,' said Jean, who had learned long ago that family arguments were rarely as contentious after they'd all been fed, 'let's eat before it all gets cold. Then we can talk about extramarital pregnancies afterwards.'

The doorbell rang.

'And here's who I'm going to have my baby with,' cried Fiona triumphantly. She jumped up and ran to open the door.

'That must be Doug,' said Jean. 'It amazes me how she knows his ring.'

'Why does he always have to come when we're having dinner?' asked Steven querulously. 'Why doesn't he stay home and take care of Cathie? Anyway, it might not be him. How can she possibly tell who it is from the sound of the bell?'

'It's not the bell,' said Lisbie mysteriously. 'It's his aura. Fiona can feel it right through the walls and doors.' She grinned swiftly at her mother, then turned to Steven. 'It's just amazing, Dad,' she said in a suggestive voice. 'Do you know where Fiona actually feels it? She says it's a kind of deep, tingly feeling . . .'

Steven, still red in the face, tightened his lips. He seemed to remember having this discussion on some previous occasion, but he refused to tolerate any kind of smutty talk from his children. 'That's quite enough from you, Lisbie,' he said sternly. 'I suggest you keep that kind of insanitary information to yourself.'

The sound of voices came through from the hall. Doug's was deep, amused, and Fiona was laughing in a bantering way. But, Lisbie wasn't about to let go. 'What do you mean, "insanitary"? *Daddy*!' her voice went up in premeditated outrage, 'Fiona feels his presence in her *heart*! Where did *you* think she felt it?'

Steven was saved from further embarrassment when Doug came into the room with Fiona hanging on to his arm.

'Evening all,' he said. 'Did I come at a bad time?'

'Of course not,' said Jean, throwing a warning glance at Steven. 'Sit down and Fiona will get you a cup of tea.'

Steven hurried through the rest of his dinner, excused himself and went upstairs to watch the news on television.

Jean and Douglas went into the living room. Fiona wanted to come with them, and was indignant when Jean asked pointedly if she had tidied her room.

'You're always trying to embarrass me, Mum,' said Fiona, but she didn't persist.

'How's Cathie doing?' asked Jean, sitting back in her armchair. Doug looked tired and irritable.

'She'll be happy when the baby comes,' he said. 'And so will I. Right now, there's hardly enough room in the bed for all three of us.'

'Well, it's only a few more weeks now,' replied Jean. 'And you can always sleep on the couch.'

'Cathie would no' like that,' grinned Douglas. 'She says she gets cold if I'm not there.'

'Did you talk to the Dalgleishes?'

'I did that,' he replied. 'That's what I wanted to talk to you about.'

Douglas moved restlessly in his chair and without

thinking took out the packet he always carried in his breast-pocket and extracted the single weary-looking cigarette in it. Noticing Jean's expression, he put it back hurriedly. 'Three months and eighteen days it's been,' he said. 'And I still dream about smoking.'

'The Dalgleishes,' said Jean, looking at the clock. She had work to do.

'They're weird.' He told Jean about his interviews. 'That Sir Colin,' he said, shaking his head, 'he's no' exactly a strong, masterful lord of the manor, is he?'

Jean sighed. 'How can I help you, Douglas?'

'The thing is, Jean, I can never get a *feel* for what's going on with people like the Dalgleishes. Now you're different, you can mix with the likes of them, no problem, and . . .'

'Do you think one of them was involved? Or was it someone from outside?'

Douglas shook his head in frustration. 'I don't know. There's a name that keeps cropping up: Rory McDermott. Do you know him?'

Jean thought for a moment. 'Yes. Well, I know his wife, Bella. She was quite ill for a while with depression, and he came in with her a couple of times . . . Oh, my . . .' Jean's hand went up to her mouth, and her voice became thoughtful. 'At the time he was working on the Dalgleish estate, and Bella was working in the kitchens. She was convinced that he was having an affair with . . . yes, you've guessed it . . . Miss Moira. Rory's a good-looking young man.'

Douglas watched Jean as she tried to recall the details of the story.

'What happened?'

'Just what you'd expect. They were caught and he was fired. Bella was sure it was Moira's fault; that she'd not only stolen her man but got him fired as well.'

'Did you remember all that just now?' enquired Douglas, surprised.

'Douglas Niven, if you heard half the stories of love

and hate I hear every day, you wouldn't remember them all either, and this happened months ago,' replied Jean sharply, but she was annoyed at her own tardy recollection.

'Do you ever get up to Dalgleish House?' asked Douglas, going off on another tack.

'No, but I'm going up with Steven and the girls on Sunday,' replied Jean. 'Elspeth Dalgleish was in the surgery with Moira's wee boy, and she asked me to visit.'

'Good.' Douglas sounded pleased. 'Maybe you can make more sense out of all of them than I.'

'Douglas, I'm not going up there to do any spying for you. We're going because it's a good opportunity for Steven and the girls to see a famous old house we wouldn't normally get to see.' Jean's voice was a shade tart. 'Now, I have about two hours' work to do, so unless there's anything else—'

'Get them to show you her bedroom,' said Douglas. 'I didn't find anything, but what's in that room is all that's really left of Moira, and maybe a woman's eye sees more in a woman's bedroom than a man's does.'

Doug was sounding so desperate that Jean laughed. 'We're going up there on a social visit, Douglas Niven,' she said. 'Maybe you should go to one of these sensitivity workshops I've been hearing about. They might give you some insight into the female mind.'

Fiona was hanging around outside in the hall, and grabbed Douglas as he came out of the living room. Doug turned his head to say goodnight to Jean, and Fiona escorted him back to his car, putting her arm through his.

PART TWO

Chapter Eleven

Bella McDermott sat in the bleak ground-floor waiting room of the main Perth police station, wondering if they were going to question her too. A very large policeman had come to their home early that morning to pick up Rory, and she insisted on going to the station with them. She had been so noisy and angry, shouting at both of them from the back seat, that Constable Jamieson had finally threatened to arrest her for breach of the peace. Bella was normally a very quiet, reticent woman, and her unusual outburst had been a cover-up for her fear, which was not only for Rory.

She got up and walked over to the window. Below, the wet, black surface of Caledonian Road slashed past the snow-covered area in front of the station, and the long lines of cars and lorries slowing for the intersection made their way cautiously along the street, squirting parabolic jets of wet, brown, slush from under their tyres when they came close to the kerb.

If they did question her, Bella wondered, what would they ask? Would they want to know what she knew about that slut Moira? What would she say to them? What about that phone call? In retrospect, that had been a serious mistake, she was aware of that. The last thing she really wanted was to draw attention to herself or Rory, but on the other hand something, some

instinct, had forced her to do it. Did she subconsciously
want Rory to suffer for having caused her so much
hurt? Was the death of Moira Dalgleish not enough to
satisfy her need to get even?

Of course, thought Bella, turning away from the
window, maybe they just wanted to talk to Rory about
the salmon poaching. Maybe they didn't even know
about him and Moira, or the fight she, Bella, had with
her when she bumped into Moira coming out of that
hairdressing place? There had been quite a row and
some good scratches had been exchanged, but luckily a
couple of people had separated them before the police
were called.

Now, Bella didn't even try to subdue her exhilaration
at the knowledge that Moira was dead. While that
creature was alive, she knew that Rory kept thinking
about her, hoping that she would come back to him.
He'd lie awake, night after night beside her, and she
knew that Moira was in his mind all the time, and both
of them were going crazy because of her.

Inside his office, Doug was sitting behind his cramped
desk, getting down to business. Rory was in the hot seat,
facing him across the desk with his back to the wall: a
symbolic touch that appealed to Doug's inquisitorial
instincts. Jamieson occupied the rest of the available
space.

'How long before her death had you known Miss
Moira?' Doug asked Rory.

Rory squirmed on the uncomfortable chair. He was a
well-built, sturdy man with untidy blond hair, and wore
an old tweed jacket. There was a self-reliant, outdoors
look about him.

'Who said I knew her? You tell me, if you know all
about it,' he retorted with an attempt at bravado.

Doug sat back, very relaxed. This was just the kind of
situation he liked, where the suspect didn't just keel
over and confess, but gave him a fight for his money.

Douglas knew the 'Rorys' of the world like the back of his hand; he knew their fears, their insecurities, and how to find and exploit their vulnerabilites. At one time in his life, as he well knew, Douglas might easily have joined them.

'McDermott,' he said, showing his widest shark-smile, 'between you and me, you're in a lot more trouble than you seem to realize.' He surveyed his victim, knowing that every petty criminal always has more to hide than just what he is being charged with. 'Now you go along with us, answer my questions proper-like, and maybe we can help you. I don't have anything against you personally. On the contrary, I'm just trying to find out what happened to Miss Moira, and I know that you can help me.'

'She lived up in the big house,' said Rory in a tight voice. 'And that's all I know.'

Doug sighed, and Jamieson, who didn't have Doug's patience, made a quick movement that Rory could have interpreted as threatening. Rory didn't flinch, but kept a wary eye on Jamieson from then on.

'Rory, I know *all* about you and Miss Moira, because you weren't very discreet, so don't waste our time. You were fired from your job because you were having an affair with her.' Doug shook his head regretfully. 'You should have known better, Rory. Stick to your own class, is what I say, and you won't get hurt so badly.'

Two red spots appeared on Rory's cheeks, but he didn't say anything.

'Didn't you know she'd give a roll in the hay to anybody? Anybody at all? I just hope you didn't catch anything you might pass on to Bella.'

Rory's lips tightened.

'I can certainly see why you might want to kill her,' said Doug in a conversational tone. 'She got tired of you and then made sure you got fired. You thought it was love; she thought it was a lark.' Douglas, watching carefully, was doing what good fortune-tellers do:

talking, and getting steered in the right direction by tiny clues from the subject's body language.

'You wanted to leave Bella and marry Moira, am I right?' Douglas's compassion was there for all to see, and Rory got the impression that Doug must have had the same kind of experience, and knew what the pain of that situation felt like. 'And Moira just laughed at you when you suggested it, didn't she?' Doug's voice expressed his solidarity; he and Rory were two men united in the face of female oppression and betrayal.

Rory licked his lips, hesitated, stared at Douglas, but still said nothing. Douglas knew he had the man almost where he wanted him.

'Leaving the lure atttached to her body was very symbolic, nae doubt,' went on Douglas, leaning sideways and fishing in his pocket for the plastic bag. 'I suppose it meant that you'd finally caught her, even if she was dead.' He took the shiny spoon lure carefully out of the bag and placed it on the desk. Rory looked at it, wide-eyed. He was afraid now.

'Go ahead, take it, Rory,' said Doug, leaning back and watching him. 'We've lifted your prints from it. We know it's yours.'

With his eyes on Douglas, Rory leaned forward, as if hypnotized, and picked up the spoon by the broken nylon leader. He had never expected to see it again.

'Now, lad,' said Douglas, satisfied when Rory had taken the lure, 'I'd like you to tell me exactly how that lure became attached to the body of Miss Moira Dalgleish.'

After Rory had told Doug his version of what had happened that night, Doug surveyed his prey. 'Rory, lad, did it ever occur to you that Bella might have done it?'

Rory's face went pasty white, and Doug knew that he had struck a bull's-eye.

At Dalgleish House, Patricia was supervising preparations for the Sunday brunch, which she and Alastair had insisted on seeing through despite querulous objections from Colin. Elspeth, accustomed to going along with anything that Alastair decided, offered no resistance. The brunch had been arranged long before, and several very important people were coming from Edinburgh, people Alastair needed to keep on good terms with if he was ever to become the political leader of a Scotland free of the yoke of English domination.

But Colin was not enthusiastic. 'For one thing,' he said, 'we can't afford this kind of entertainment, and surely, this is not the time . . .' He turned to appeal to his wife. 'Isn't that so, Elspeth? You tell him; he doesn't listen to me.'

'There's not much we can do now, Colin,' answered Elspeth, biting nervously on her fingernail. 'There isn't enough time to cancel. Anyway, it'll be nice. There'll be some new people to meet, and the Foremans are coming, you remember Denis and Ilona, I know you like them. Then there's the Montroses, and some of Alastair's important political friends. In any case, dear, it isn't going to cost that much.' Elspeth glanced at Alastair, who was paying the bill for the party, and he nodded rather distantly. Patricia took Elspeth's arm and went down to the kitchens. Patricia was used to directing operations, and preferred situations where people didn't argue with her. The kitchen was such a place. Emily might scowl, or even glower, but she never argued.

Both men listened to their wives' footsteps as they diminished towards the end of the corridor. Then Alastair went over to the door and closed it gently.

'Colin, now's as good a time as any, I suppose . . .' he looked uncertainly at his brother, who, sensing a discussion, had sat down and curled up in the sofa again. His eyes were closed tight, as if to shut out all the unpleasant things in the entire world.

'Colin, we're going to be leaving early on Monday. I have a speech to make at the Guildhall . . .'

'You and your politics!' said Colin in his usual petulant way. 'Suppose you *do* become the first Prime Minister of Scotland, then what? Will that turn you into a happy, contented man?'

Two pink spots appeared on Alastair's cheeks. His sense of humour did not extend to discussion of his political aspirations. 'If you would take a little more interest in politics yourself,' he snapped, 'then this house and all the family land might be in less parlous shape. One of the factors that has ruined this family has been death duties and taxes of all kinds that go to line the pockets of the English in Whitehall. The other factor, Colin, if you don't mind my saying so again, is your incredible incompetence when it comes to running the estate's affairs. I would like to suggest, once more, that you allow me to take over and manage—'

'No!' Colin sat up straight. 'Alastair, we've been through this *so* many times. We have a responsibility to our tenants, and I refuse to sell the land from under them. Any of it. It's terrible of you to bring this up again, especially now that Moira . . . that Moira . . .' Colin put his head in his hands and started to sob again.

Alastair watched his brother with a mixture of affection and contempt. Ever since Colin was a child, he had resorted to tears to get his own way or to avoid responsibility, but in the last couple of years he'd been getting worse. He's like a woman, thought Alastair, although in the same breath he recognized that the women around him were made of much stronger stuff than Colin.

Well, thought Alastair, rather sadly, plan one didn't work, again. I'm afraid the time is fast approaching for plan two.

Elspeth appeared at the door. Despite years of living on and off in the same house with him, she always managed to startle Alastair by materializing where he was, apparently without having gone through the process of getting there; he hadn't heard any approaching footsteps in the corridor, which resonated emptily to the steps of everyone else.

'Damn it, Elspeth,' he grumbled, 'I wish you'd stop creeping up on me like that. You're the only ghost I've ever met who hasn't had to die before making an appearance.'

Elspeth said nothing, but went over to Colin, who was collapsed, once again, on the couch.

'Our guests should be arriving in about an hour,' she said gently to him, lightly massaging the back of his neck.

Colin groaned. 'I'm staying here,' he said. 'Don't let them in.'

To most people, it would have seemed that Elspeth had not changed in any way over the last few days, but Alastair, who knew her well, detected an almost imperceptible increase in her self-confidence, a reduction of her terrible self-doubt and insecurity, and he wondered what could have caused it.

Chapter Twelve

'Mum, do we *have* to go?' When Jean had first announced the invitation, Fiona had been enthusiastic about going to Dalgleish House but, as usual, when the time came she had planned other things. 'And anyway,' she said, 'I'm tired of seeing how rich people live.'

'Of course you don't have to come, dear,' said Jean, 'but it would be a perfect opportunity to wear your new red dress.'

That did it. Fiona thought for a second, ran upstairs and reappeared moments later, looking most attractive in a pretty dark-red wool dress with black trimmings that she had bought with her Christmas money.

Steven could usually be counted on to grumble and balk before an outing he had not organized, but today he seemed actually to be looking forward to it.

'Come on, everybody,' he called up the stairs. 'All the food'll be gone if we don't hurry.'

Most of the snow had melted off the main road, but Steven could see there was still some on the sheltered driveway of Dalgleish House. The big granite pillars had long since lost their gates; sold, it was said, to an American rock-and-roll star.

'Not as fancy as Strathalmond Castle, is it?' said Lisbie, remembering a former outing. The driveway was deeply rutted, and Steven drove his Rover on the edge of the road to avoid the bumps. There was a sudden thud on the car roof that startled all of them, but it was only wet snow falling from the branches above them.

'There's something creepy about this place,' said Lisbie, always very sensitive to atmosphere. She shivered.

'Scary,' said Fiona in a hushed whisper. 'Oh, Lisbie,' she cried suddenly, 'look! There's something going up your leg! It's a spider!'

Lisbie screamed, and the Rover swerved, almost going into the trees at the side of the narrow drive.

'For heaven's sake!' said Steven angrily, unable to look behind him as he struggled to get the car out of the particularly deep rut it had lurched into. 'What's going on back there?'

Lisbie, panicking, had her skirt up around her waist, and Fiona was laughing at the trick she'd played on her sister. She had a dread of spiders and other creepy-crawlies, and Fiona always knew exactly the moment to get her.

'It doesn't bother *you*,' she said angrily to Fiona, 'because you have so many insects up between your legs you don't even notice.'

'I'd forgotten how huge your legs are, Lisbie,' retorted Fiona in a wondering tone. 'That poor spider must have felt like it was crossing the Sahara. Oh, there it is!'

Lisbie screamed again, and half stood up, shaking her skirt and looking on the seat for the non-existent arachnid. By this time Steven was really furious, and it took Jean's calm reassurance that no spider was within a hundred yards of them before Lisbie settled down.

'I'll get you for this later,' she said to Fiona.

Order had been more or less restored by the time they pulled up outside the front portico, but Lisbie was still shaken.

There were a couple of cars in front of the house, a long, two-storey building, flanked by extending wings on both sides of a large square-fronted house. Steven pulled up outside the porticoed front door, and Jean, stepping out into the damp air, noticed a high gutter hanging down from the roof, broken off, she assumed, by the weight of the recent snowfalls. There was something sad and unkempt about the place. It made Jean think of one of her patients, an old man who had worked hard all his life, but, now ill, had given up hope and ambition, and was waiting only to die.

Elspeth Dalgleish appeared at the front door, wearing a simple dark-green woollen dress and low-heeled shoes. Steven let his passengers out, then drove over to park on the opposite side of the courtyard next to the two other cars. He stepped out straight into a slushy puddle, which did nothing to improve his already frazzled state of mind.

A nephew of the Dalgleishes was there for the day from Edinburgh, a good-looking young man with shoulder-length blond hair, an ear-ring in one earlobe and the brightest of blue eyes. Steven observed him with secret distaste, but both Fiona and Lisbie fell instantly in love with him, and after a few moments the three of them went off to look at the horses.

Alastair, happy to find a potential voter, led a reluctant Steven into the huge, draughty, main reception room to talk politics, and Elspeth, whom Jean suspected of having arranged the dispersion of the Montrose clan, led Jean up the stairs and along a bleak corridor to her living room. It was a surprisingly pleasant room, with bright chintz-covered easy chairs, an old but beautiful desk with lots of drawers with square-cut brass handles, and a big window that looked out over the back of the house, the snow-speckled kitchen garden and through the dark, wintry trees. Jean caught a brief glimpse of the service cottages and the black river beyond them before Elspeth sat her down. From somewhere in the house came the sound of a baby crying.

'How is he doing, the wee bairn?' asked Jean, with motherly interest.

'I'm sending him away to stay with relatives in Edinburgh,' said Elspeth. 'They have a couple of children, and he'll be better off there.'

Jean had to agree.

'We have a little time to talk before the guests arrive,' said Elspeth, smiling, giving the impression that Jean was part of the family rather one of the guests. Her expression became sombre. 'I know that you've been involved in a few *events* around Perth, Jean,' she said. 'We knew the Lumsdens, and, of course, Marina Strathalmond is a close friend of mine. Actually she was the one who suggested I talk to you.'

'Oh dear,' said Jean, embarrassed. 'It was just by chance that I got involved in those cases, and anyway right now I'm so busy with my practice that—'

'Jean, I'm really concerned about Colin.' Elspeth's voice was low and intense, and Jean was startled. 'He's getting more and more absent-minded, he weeps at the slightest thing, and he flies into dreadful rages. I hope that didn't . . . Of course, Moira's death has made him worse. We have no money, and Alastair's been trying to persuade Colin to sell some of our property near Dunfermline, but he just refuses. Jean, I've decided to take him to Switzerland, to the Lange Clinic in Geneva. They specialize in nervous conditions . . .' Elspeth's voice faded, then came back again. 'I spent money I didn't have to take him to Harley Street, but they couldn't tell me what was the matter with him, or what to do to help him. Poor Colin . . .'

There was a knock on the door and Colin came in, unshaven, shuffling in a old maroon dressing-gown tied with a tasselled cord.

'Oh, I didn't know you had a visitor,' he said, standing in the doorway and evidently put out.

'This is my husband Colin,' said Elspeth, a touch of

colour on her cheeks. 'Colin, have you met Dr Montrose?'

'I've heard of you,' said Colin, looking at Jean. His voice was high-pitched, irritable. 'In fact, I was thinking of coming to see you. Professionally, I mean.'

He came further into the room and sat down. Elspeth glanced resignedly at Jean.

'Were you talking about Moira?'

'Not exactly,' replied Elspeth. 'We were—'

'I think you should look into it,' he said to Jean. 'The police don't seem to know what . . .' His voice faded, and he looked over at Elspeth as if he'd lost track of what he was saying.

'What to do,' said Elspeth, used to finishing her husband's sentences.

Jean remembered Doug's plea for her to look at Moira's bedroom, but she still felt reluctant to suggest it.

Colin stood up in a sudden rage, his eyes bulging and his fists clenched. Alarmed, Jean gripped the sides of her chair. At that moment Sir Colin was quite frightening, and out of the corner of her eye she saw Elspeth flinch.

'They left fingerprint powder everywhere and moved her things all around,' he said. 'They didn't really give a damn about her, about Moira as a person . . .' Tears flew into his eyes, and he sat down again, all his pathological energy evaporating in an instant.

Startled by a thought that had just come into her mind, Jean stood up. 'Would you like me to take a look at Moira's rooms?' she asked. 'I can't promise it'll do any good, but at least . . .' Jean put a sympathetic hand on Colin's arm, 'at least I promise not to leave any fingerprint powder.'

In fact, Moira's room had scarcely been disturbed by Doug and his team, and Jean had to look carefully at the door and bedside table to find the powder Colin had been so bitter about.

She surveyed the living room from the doorway, and tried to get an impression of the woman who had lived there; a young, vibrant, lively person, shaken by the death of her husband, and left with a baby to care for.

'Was that Mr Glashan?' asked Jean, pointing at the framed photograph.

'Yes,' replied Elspeth. 'Actually, the only one of us who ever met him was Alastair, down in London.'

Jean stepped into the room and went over to look at the portrait. It was a studio shot, with good back-lighting that showed his strong and extremely handsome features. 'They must have been quite a pair,' said Jean, thinking how dashing the two of them would have looked walking into a restaurant. She picked up the frame and gazed at the picture. Two young, beautiful people, and both dead. The signature on the picture was illegible, and the name of the studio was printed in gold letters at the bottom, so small that Jean had to put on her reading glasses to read it.

'Do you mind if I take it out of the frame?' asked Jean. 'I'll be very careful.'

She undid the holding clips, hoping that there might be another picture under it, maybe one of both of them together. There was nothing there besides the portrait and the backing cardboard. The only thing she hadn't already seen was a smudged studio number, stamped on the back of the print.

Aside from the cot and a couple of toys on the floor, the bedroom looked as if Moira had grown up in it, as indeed she had. On the walls there were old posters of rock concerts in Germany, America, and France; and on the dresser stood a pretty ceramic ballerina with a pink tutu. 'She spins around,' said Elspeth, dry-eyed, 'when the mechanism is wound up. There was a time when Moira had wanted to be a ballerina. That was the year before she decided to be a horse trainer . . .'

Gingerly, Jean picked up the figurine and glanced at the base. Written in Indian ink on the bottom were the words: *To the next Margot Fonteyn, with love from Alastair and Patricia.*

There were many more small ornaments: carved wooden boxes; bric-à-brac; dolls of various sizes and shapes. Each one had been given to Moira by someone or other, and, remarkably, Elspeth seemed to remember every person who had presented her daughter with a gift or souvenir. School friends, former lovers identified only by an initial, Elspeth recalled each one, until Jean pointed at a hand-carved wooden model of a salmon, crafted with care and painted with familiarity rather than skill.

'Who gave her that?' asked Jean.

'I don't remember.' Suddenly losing interest in the knick-knacks, Elspeth went over to the wardrobe and opened the door. 'Here, Jean, we haven't even looked at her clothes. Moira's tastes were, I suppose you might say, *eclectic.*'

Indeed, there was a bit of everything; a rack of dresses from Givenchy and Armani, sad and spiritless on their hangers, like corpses suspended from hooks. There were silk scarves from Hermès and Gucci, and a whole stack of T-shirts with logos representing everything from Mickey Mouse to anti-nuclear demonstrations.

According to Elspeth, Alastair had spoiled Moira and had bought most of the dresses; the T-shirts were mainly Christmas and birthday presents, because everybody knew she collected them.

As they left the room, Jean asked if anything there had been given to Moira by her husband.

'As far as I know,' said Elspeth, closing the door behind them, 'all he ever gave her was a wedding ring and a baby.'

The door opposite was half-open, revealing what looked like a spacious office; Jean asked who worked there.

'Alastair,' replied Elspeth, and before she had time to close the door, Jean had walked in. It was a big room, with a table, a telephone, and a small computer console on the desk. An entire wall was covered with grey filing cabinets, all with new-looking heavy padlocks on them.

Elspeth caught Jean's glance. 'Oh, he's an obsessive record-keeper,' she said. 'I've never seen them, but apparently he's kept records about everything he has ever done, from his kindergarten report cards to the names of people he talks to at constituents' meetings.'

Jean laughed. On top of one of the filing cabinets was a framed colour photograph of Alastair and Moira, apparently on a mountain top, their hair blowing in the wind.

'They used to go hiking a lot,' explained Elspeth. 'Especially when Moira was younger.' Colin appeared at the door, still in his dressing-gown, and Elspeth looked at her watch. 'Our guests should be arriving soon, Colin,' she said gently. 'Don't you think you should go and shave and get dressed?'

Chapter Thirteen

'All right then, Bella,' said Jamieson in his move-right-along-there voice. He poked his big square face around the waiting room door, 'Kindly step this way. It's your turn now.'

Bella felt her heart sink into her boots, but she got up. Walking down the corridor in the opposite direction, she saw her husband, accompanied by a uniformed officer. Rory turned, and she caught a glimpse of his face before the policeman hustled him along. He looked pale and scared.

'Did you arrest him?' she asked Jamieson in a shrill voice. 'Because he never—'

'Relax, Bella. He's just going out the back way. Now you step in here.'

Douglas was sitting behind his desk in the cramped office, and when Bella entered he pointed at the empty chair against the wall. 'Have a seat, Bella. Would you like a cup of tea? Or coffee?'

Bella stared sullenly at him and shook her head.

'I'm not saying nothing,' she said.

Ignoring the double negative, Douglas replied mildly that he hadn't asked her anything, not yet, anyway, and all he wanted was for her to confirm a couple of things that Rory had said. If she could do that, he implied, that would be the end of the matter and she could go home.

Douglas settled back in his chair, and surveyed Bella benignly.

'Let's go back to when you were working for Lady Dalgleish,' he said. 'When was that, exactly?'

Jamieson opened his notebook, fixed his eyes on Bella and held the chewed stub of his pencil at the ready.

'I worked there for about four years,' replied Bella, feeling a sour flutter in her stomach. 'What's that got to do with the price of tea?'

'Were you employed as a maid?' asked Doug.

'They don't have no maids up there,' said Bella contemptuously. 'They don't have enough money. I worked in the kitchen and did some cleaning.'

'Why did you leave?'

'Because of Emily McNab, the cook. She hated me.'

'Now, Bella,' said Douglas, smiling indulgently, 'you don't have to be ashamed of what happened. In your shoes, I would have done the same thing mysel'.'

Bella stared at him, trying to decide how much he knew. He had such a confident, relaxed manner that, mentally, she threw in the towel; Rory must have told him everything.

'She was making him crazy,' she said. 'All he could think about was her. Moira, Moira, Moira.' Bella spat the name out. 'It would have been different if she'd loved him, but she was just playing with him, he was like a toy that she threw away when she got tired of it.'

'What actually happened?'

'We were living together in the cottage on the estate, him and me,' said Bella. 'Then something happened, she did something, I still don't know what it was, but from then on Rory forgot about me. He wouldn't even talk. Emily told me what was going on, so I went straight up to talk to Moira. That was just before she went off to get married, the bitch, although I certainly didn't know it at the time.' Bella's lips compressed, and she clasped her hands together in her lap. She had big hands for a woman, Doug noticed.

'So, what happened?'

'She was surprised to see me, I suppose. She laughed and told me that Rory was no great shakes as a lover, and I could have him back.'

'Then?'

'Then I went back downstairs and told Emily I was leaving.'

Douglas shook his head. 'Now, Bella. That may be the truth, but it isn't the whole truth, is it? Tell me what really happened.'

Bella looked at her hands. 'I lost my temper,' she answered in a low voice. 'I hit her. I slapped her face . . .'

Doug waited, but Bella said no more. 'According to information I have received, Bella,' said Douglas heavily, 'the reason you were fired was because you attempted to strangle Moira Dalgleish after an argument, and she had to wear a scarf for ten days to hide the marks on her neck.'

'She deserved it,' said Bella, looking up defiantly. 'And I'd do it again.'

'We'll go into *that* later,' said Douglas, with a significant tap on his desk. Jamieson was writing furiously and starting to breathe heavily. Doug recognized the signs and waited for him to catch up.

'Now, Bella, let's you and me talk about Rory for a minute,' he said, shifting in his chair as if all that unfortunate business between Bella and Moira had been disposed of. 'You see, I'm afraid he's the one who's really in trouble.'

The other guests were arriving at Dalgleish House by the time Jean had examined Moira's rooms and talked about her to her parents. Colin hadn't said much, but had stayed close to Elspeth, preventing her from talking to Jean alone. Eventually, Elspeth addressed him sternly, as she would a child, 'Colin, our guests are here. Either you go and dress and shave then come and join the party, or you go back to your rooms.'

Colin decided to join the party, and shuffled off to
get ready. Jean watched him receding down the
corridor. He stumbled a couple of times.

Elspeth had just started to tell Jean what was on her
mind when Emily arrived on the scene, all hot and
bothered. There was nobody to welcome the guests, she
said. They were all standing around uncomfortably,
waiting in the great hall.

Elspeth became flustered again, and hurried down the
corridor, accompanied by a muttering Emily and
followed by Jean, whose mind was full of the things
she'd just seen and not understood, and puzzled by both
Elspeth and Colin, in entirely different ways.

Alastair and Patricia had appeared and were greeting
the guests, among whom were several well-known
figures, a couple of whom Jean recognized from
television. One was the Scottish Secretary, urbane,
white-haired, with a wife to match in an electric-blue
silk dress, and the other was a middle-aged member of
the Cabinet, who kept obsessively touching his young
wife. Alastair had worked at one time with both men,
and afterwards they stood together in a group in the
corner, talking, telling jokes, recalling people and
events while their wives tried to think of something to
say to each other. Patricia circulated like a queen,
gracious, poised, elegant, never stopping long with any
one guest, making sure that everyone had a drink and
somebody to talk to. Elspeth tucked herself unobtru-
sively in a corner and watched.

Steven went around, valiantly trying to talk to the
other guests, but most of them just looked right through
him, until finally he went off in search of his daughters.
Jean circulated, chatting happily with one and all.

Colin, even after he had shaved and dressed, looked
much the same as before, and burst into tears on two
occasions when Moira's name was sympathetically
brought up.

Steven found Fiona and Lisbie listening entranced to the Dalgleish nephew who was playing a guitar. Steven detached them with some difficulty, and not before they exchanged phone numbers and addresses with him, then went back to find Jean, who was listening rather restrainedly to Ilona and Denis Foreman, a handsome couple whom Jean knew but hadn't seen for some months.

'We're leaving,' Steven announced rather abruptly to the small group, and a few minutes later they were all in the Rover, the girls complaining that for once they had been having the *best* time of their entire lives and why did Daddy *always* have to spoil it? Jean was not too pleased either, although it was more the manner in which she had been plucked from the party that annoyed her. In the face of Fiona's and Lisbie's remonstrances, however, she decided not to say anything about it, and made an attempt to divert the conversation.

'He seemed a nice young man, the nephew,' she said. That did it. Both her daughters sang his praises simultaneously, and Jean learned that not only was young Ken Dalgleish a mathematical genius, attending Oxford mainly as a favour to the faculty and fellows, but he was also a guitarist who made Andrés Segovia sound like a raw beginner.

'God, he's so beautiful,' sighed Fiona. 'Lisbie, did you notice his hands? They were so . . .' For once, Fiona was at a loss for words.

'Elegant?' suggested Jean.

'Yes, but much *more* than that,' said Fiona.

'Some of his toes were joined together,' said Lisbie admiringly.

'Just the last two,' said Fiona. 'I don't know why, but on him it looked very sexy.'

Steven hurrumphed warningly. That kind of conversation had to be nipped in the bud before it got out of hand. Then he caught his breath. 'How do you happen

to know that about his toes?' he asked sharply,
wondering if there had been some kind of orgy out there
in the stables.

'He was wearing thongs,' said Lisbie giggling. 'I bet
you thought we'd all got undressed together, didn't you,
Daddy?'

'I wish,' murmured Fiona, her voice pitched just loud
enough for Steven to hear.

'Why would they be joined like that, Mum? I mean
his toes,' asked Lisbie.

'The Dalgleish men all have it, apparently,' replied
Jean. 'Which reminds me, did either of you see the
baby?'

'For a second,' said Fiona. 'He was all bundled up
and Emily gave him to a woman who came for him in a
car. Emily said he'd be safer away from the house.'

'Oh my,' said Jean, startled. It hadn't occurred to her
that Moira's baby might be in danger. Others in that
household, perhaps, but surely not the baby. Jean had a
momentary flashback about little Magnus Lumsden and
shuddered.

Then she had another guilty twinge; there was no
doubt that Elspeth's invitation had been so she could
talk to her about what had happened to Moira, and
about her anxieties concerning her own safety. For one
reason or another, Elspeth had barely been able to say
that she felt in danger, and Jean knew that she hadn't
helped very much. She could quite easily have taken
Elspeth aside at some point and allowed her to explain
what she was afraid of.

Always as honest with herself as with everyone else,
Jean recognized that she didn't feel very comfortable
with Elspeth. There was something about her that made
Jean unwilling to listen to her confidences, even when
they concerned the murder of her daughter.

The telephone was ringing when they got home. It
was Douglas, calling from the hospital. Cathie was in
labour, had been taken there by ambulance, and, he

said, Dr McIntosh was very concerned about her.

'I'll be right over,' said Jean.

Chapter Fourteen

The maternity unit at the hospital was on the second floor, and Jean was so concerned about Cathie that, unwisely, she ran up the stairs instead of taking the lift. At the top, she leaned against the banister, out of breath and faint from the exertion. She stood there panting for a couple of minutes, wishing that somebody had put a chair at the head of the stairs, and telling herself that really she had to lose some weight and start taking exercise every day.

Douglas, white as a sheet, was sitting in the sister's room. Sister Elsie Duguid and Dr McIntosh were with Cathie, he told her, and they'd been there for a while.

Cathie was looking better than Doug, but still not great.

'How's the baby doing?' Jean asked Peter McIntosh, while putting a comforting hand on Cathie's shoulder. Cathie smiled; seeing Jean made her feel better than any fancy treatment the others could give her.

'We've got the foetal monitor on her,' said Peter cautiously. 'So far, the baby seems all right. Cathie's suffered a small haemorrhage and isn't dilating well. She's a breech, probably with an oligohydramnios.'

Cathie rolled her eyes at Jean. 'That sounds seriously fatal,' she said, trying to be brave, but Jean could see that she was really scared.

'Breech is just a way of saying that the baby's trying to come out bottom first,' said Jean, her matter-of-fact voice very comforting to Cathie, 'and the oligo bit means there isn't quite as much fluid as they'd like around the baby.'

'We tried to do an external version,' said Peter. He glanced at Cathie. 'That's the medical name for turning the baby around, what we were trying to do a wee while ago.' Peter addressed Jean again. 'The version didn't work. We have an additional problem because she has a small pelvis and there's some disproportion.'

'I think Dr McIntosh is getting around to saying you're going to need a Caesarean,' said Jean, looking at Peter, who nodded.

Cathie shrugged. 'I've waited for years for this baby,' she said, 'and I'm tired of waiting. If you need to do a Caesarean, let's get on with it.' Cathie grabbed Jean's hand so tightly it hurt. 'You'll be there, won't you?' she asked, her eyes fixed on Jean's. 'While he's doing it? Promise?'

'Of course,' replied Jean. 'What about Doug? Nowadays nobody minds the fathers coming in, do they, Peter?'

'No thanks,' said Cathie emphatically before Peter could respond. 'The lad would faint, likely, and anyway,' she hesitated, 'I just don't want him to see me like that. You understand, Jean, don't you?'

'Yes, I do,' said Jean, thinking back to when she had her girls. The idea of Steven actually coming into the delivery room while she was in labour was next to unthinkable.

The Sister went off to get some medicine for Cathie while Peter and Jean went to tell Douglas what was happening.

In his usual careful and methodical way, Peter started to tell him what the situation was, but after a minute Doug interrupted politely. 'Dr McIntosh, I only have one question. Does Dr Montrose agree that the Caesarean is necessary?'

They both looked at Jean.

'I'm afraid so,' said Jean.

'That's all I want to know,' replied Doug. 'Do I have to sign anything?'

Armand Thierry sat in the small office of his salon, long after everyone else had gone home, and considered the situation he was in. On the wall behind him were his diplomas from the *Ecole de Beauté* in Paris, the Los Angeles Institute of Glamorology, and two others, all forgeries. Armand's real name was Roger Van Polt, and he had come to Scotland from South Africa via Mozambique, Mexico City, where he underwent plastic surgery, and Quebec, where he worked in a salon, learned his trade, some French, and polished up his new identity.

Four years before, he had returned from a weekend sailing trip off Cape Town in his small yacht, minus his wealthy wife, who, he reported, had fallen overboard in rough weather. Her body was found by a group of drunken deep-sea fishermen, who managed to haul the body on board and brought her back to Cape Town in the freezer. An autopsy showed that she had been murdered, and when the police came for him, Roger Van Polt had already disappeared. He had taken the precaution of salting away enough of his wife's money to last him a couple of years, cover the expenses of remodelling his face, pay for the necessary bribes and documents, and set up in business. Armand had been in the cosmetic industry in South Africa, importing and wholesaling a wide range of beauty products, so his choice of a new business was not too difficult. The choice of a location was more of a problem; fortunately for him, he had a contact in Britain who secured immigration papers for him, and he had decided on

Perth after travelling around Britain for a month,
because it was a quiet town of the right size, didn't have
many first-rate beauty salons, and there was just
something about the area that appealed to him.

And now, things seemed to be unravelling. Eighteen
months before, everything was going smoothly for him.
Business was booming, he had opened a second salon in
Dundee and a third in Forfar, and was getting
concerned that he might be doing too well, because the
last thing he wanted to do was attract attention. Then
one day a good-looking blonde had come into the salon
for a haircut and a manicure. She had flirted with him,
and they had developed a rather casual intimate
relationship. She would appear at his apartment, they'd
go to bed for a while, then she'd leave. They didn't talk
much. One evening as she was getting dressed, she
casually mentioned that she knew who he was, and in
spite of his amused denials, it was clear that she did, but
he was never able to find the source of her information.
Some days later, she mentioned that she had some
unusually high expenses, and asked if he would help.
Armand gave her a hefty amount. The woman was
obviously not a professional blackmailer, and seemed to
have no intention of divulging his identity to anyone.
She'd come in every month or so, he'd give her some
money, then she'd stopped coming, and Armand was
hugely relieved to hear that she'd gone off to get
married. When she reappeared about a year later, she
came back to him, but now she was considerably
tougher. She'd still go to bed with him occasionally, but
that had nothing to do with the money she demanded on
a more regular basis. Quite aside from the blackmail,
Armand was sure that she rather liked him.

And now that she was dead, Armand thought his
troubles were finally over, then her mother appeared on
the scene, and he was back in the same jam he'd been in
before. She'd wanted to sell him his folder, but Armand
had been around the block a couple of times and knew

now these things worked. Sooner or later, she'd need more money and she'd be back. Armand was well aware that if he didn't pay her, a woman in Elspeth's position could certainly have him investigated, just by saying a word in the right ear, and he knew an investigation would be fatal, although he'd covered his tracks well.

A red fury came over him. Everything he'd accomplished was now in danger, and he knew that once again he would have to do something radical to allow him to go on living in peace. But he knew one thing for sure; whatever happened, he would never go back to South Africa to stand trial and face certain conviction. He would rather die than undergo that. With his fingers, Armand felt the slight bulge in the soft flesh of his left armpit. It was a glass ampoule containing hydrocyanic acid. It had been implanted by the surgeon in Mexico City at the same time he had had his plastic surgery. If there was no other way out, he knew he would use it.

Chapter Fifteen

Alastair Dalgleish stood by the door with Patricia, watching the last of the guests drive away.

There was a noise behind them, and they turned to see Colin lying curled up on the floor near the foot of the stairs, weeping, his face red and tear streaked. Elspeth was standing by him, looking helpless and scared.

For a moment, Alastair thought Colin had fallen down the stairs, then he shrugged and said to Patricia in a resigned voice, 'He's having one of his attacks.'

They both came in to help Elspeth.

'Has he had his medicine?' Alastair asked.

'This morning,' replied Elspeth. 'It doesn't seem to be doing him much good.'

Colin sat up. 'What are you all staring at?' he asked irritably. Alastair and Elspeth helped him to stand up. He was trembling. 'I don't feel well,' he said, and the tears welled up in his eyes again. He turned and went slowly up the stairs, supporting himself with the help of the banister.

'He's really getting worse,' said Alastair to the two women when Colin was out of earshot. 'I talked to a doctor in Edinburgh about him, and he's going to come and see him, if that's all right with you, Elspeth, of course.'

'What kind of doctor?' she asked, watching her brother-in-law.

'A consultant who specializes in nervous disorders,' replied Alastair, but he didn't look her in the eye.

'You mean a psychiatrist? He's already seen one in London.' Elspeth didn't dare tell them about the Lange Clinic; they'd want to know where she got the money to take him there. So she said, rather desperately, 'Actually, I was going to take him to see Dr Montrose. Everybody says she's very good.'

'I've heard that, too,' said Alastair. 'But Dr Patel's a specialist in this kind of problem, and, to be quite frank, Elspeth, if Colin gets worse, I think he may have to receive in-patient treatment.'

Elspeth thought about that for a moment, forced to come to grips with a situation she had been trying to avoid for many months. 'I suppose you're right,' she said finally, and with the most profound sadness. 'Poor Colin, he certainly can't go on like this.'

'When is he coming, Alastair? I mean the doctor?' asked Patricia. She put a comforting hand on Elspeth's arm. Elspeth stiffened but didn't move.

'The psychiatrist? Tomorrow. He's going to phone in the morning before he leaves his clinic.'

Patricia drew in her breath suddenly. 'Who's that?' she asked, pointing through the window.

They all looked.

'I believe it's that policeman,' said Alastair, recognizing Jamieson's bulk passing between the trees, apparently heading for the river bank. Alastair flushed with annoyance. 'What the devil is he doing back here?' He strode towards the door and called out to him. Jamieson, just within hearing range, stopped, turned and waved, then, when Alastair summoned him, walked reluctantly back towards the house.

'Do you realize that you're trespassing?' said Alastair in a crisp voice. 'Unless you happen to be in possession of a search warrant.'

'Oh no, sir,' replied Jamieson, astonished. 'I was just trying to see if Miss Moira's body could have been dropped in the river up here, and maybe floated with the current down to where it was found.'

'Where's Inspector Niven? He was distinctly told . . . Anyway, Constable, I don't think you'll find anything of interest up here, and I suggest you return to your duties in Perth. And have Inspector Niven telephone me as soon as possible.'

'Well, sir,' said Jamieson in his slow way, 'the Inspector is no' available at this time because he's about to have a baby . . . I mean, his wife Cathie is, and as a result . . .'

Alastair closed the door, leaving Jamieson still trying to explain why Doug was unobtainable.

'Damned interfering idiots,' said Alastair. 'I wish they'd spend their time finding out who killed Moira and why, and stop bothering us up here.'

'Maybe they think it was somebody here who did it,' said Patricia.

Alastair shrugged. 'I think we all know better than that, don't we?'

'I'm going upstairs to pack,' said Patricia. 'What time do you want to leave tomorrow, Alastair?'

'After the doctor-chap's been here, I suppose,' he said, unhappily. 'I really don't know what else we can do about Colin.'

Jean had been at Cathie's bedside for only a few minutes, talking with Peter McIntosh and Sister Duguid when without warning the alarm buzzer on the foetal monitor went off, and Cathie grabbed Jean's hand again. Cathie didn't say anything, and obviously wasn't in any pain or distress, but her eyes showed that she was frightened.

Peter quickly pulled out his stethoscope and put the bell on her swollen abdomen. He listened for only a few moments.

'Get the paediatrician on call,' he said to Sister Duguid in a low voice. 'Ask him to come in right away.' He turned to Cathie. 'I'm sorry, dear,' he said, 'we're going to have to do that Caesarean sooner than I thought. The baby's heart has slowed, and we need to get him out of there as soon as we can.'

'Him?' asked Cathie, bewildered.

'Him or her,' he replied, rather abruptly. 'It doesn't matter.'

Within minutes Peter and Jean were hurrying Cathie's stretcher through the corridors towards the operating theatre, with Douglas bringing up the rear of the little procession. Peter watched the monitor. The baby's heart was still running at a dangerously slow rate, and showed no signs of returning to normal.

'What do you think caused it?' asked Jean, panting a little. She was still holding Cathie's hand, and was having trouble keeping up with the stretcher.

'We'll soon find out,' replied Peter, and Jean knew that he hadn't the faintest idea either.

They went straight into the theatre, and a nurse helped to position Cathie on the table while Peter changed hurriedly into greens and started to scrub.

Anna McKenzie, the anaesthetist on call, was waiting, put in an IV, gave Cathie a quick dose of pentothal, then a short-acting muscle relaxant before inserting an endotracheal tube so that they could control her breathing.

'Peter, the baby's heart has stopped!' she called out, and Peter came running out of the scrub room, pulling on a pair of gloves and grabbing a scapel from the sterile-tray. There was no sign of the paediatrician, so Jean ran to wash her hands so that she could help.

Within two minutes Peter had opened Cathie's belly, made a transverse cut in the uterus, pushed his hand in and pulled out the baby.

'Oh my God!' said Peter, horrified. The umbilical cord was wrapped tightly around the baby's neck. As fast as he could, he tried to unwind it, but at that moment Cathie's uterus started to haemorrhage. He hardly knew what to do first, then Jean reappeared. Peter's hands were shaking, but within seconds he clamped the cord and cut it, then handed the baby over to Jean before turning back to deal with Cathie's haemorrhage which was threatening to become uncontrollable.

Without even putting the baby in the bassinet, Jean struggled to unwind the cord from around his neck, but it had been tightly coiled and even when she had freed his neck there seemed to be no life in the baby. His face was blue, and he didn't kick or move his arms. The nurse tried to find a pulse but without success.

'Suction!' Jean took the tube and sucked the mucus out of the baby's mouth before applying her own mouth to the baby's and starting to give him artificial respiration. With her hand on his tiny chest she compressed it regularly, trying to start the heart beating again, but without success.

'Give me a baby laryngoscope and an endotracheal tube,' she said to the nurse, 'the smallest you've got.' She tried to keep her voice calm, but she could feel her own heart pounding hard inside her chest.

Jean hadn't done this for years, but she took the curved blade, switched the light on and put it inside the baby's mouth. By sheer chance, she was able to see the vocal cords and Jean pushed the tube between them. 'It's in!' she said, then blew into the other end of the tube to inflate his lungs.

'How's it going, Jean?' asked Peter, desperately agitated that he couldn't help her, but he was having trouble controlling the bleeding from Cathie's uterus and couldn't turn away even for a moment to see what was going on.

Jean, too busy to answer, kept blowing and pushing on the chest. She knew she had to be careful not to fracture the baby's delicate ribs and breastbone, and as the minutes ticked away, she felt her own heart contracting. The baby remained blue and floppy, without any sign of life, but she didn't let up on her efforts, and persisted with a fierce determination that gave her the extra energy to go on.

'There still isn't a heartbeat,' said the nurse, watching the monitor. She was very experienced, and would have already given up if she had been in charge, but she was hesitant to suggest that to Jean.

Jean was exhausted, and almost ready to abandon her efforts when there was a flicker on the screen, and the baby's heartbeat reappeared, slow, irregular, but unmistakable.

The door opened and Dr Craig, the paediatrician, ran in, and between breaths into the baby's mouth, Jean told him what was happening. For the next twenty minutes the two of them worked desperately hard, inflating the lungs, trying to get the tiny heart to function. They gave oxygen and Dr Craig put a tiny needle into a scalp vein so they could give intravenous medications. Gradually the heartbeat strengthened, quickened, and the baby's awful grey-blue colour changed to a mottled pink, and after what seemed an eternity, the baby was finally breathing on his own, and his heart was strong and steady at one hundred and twenty beats per minute.

They all stood there, panting with exertion, not yet daring to feel any sense of accomplishment. The baby was far from being out of the woods.

A little later, when the situation had further stabilized, Dr Craig decided to take a chance and take the tube out of the baby's windpipe. They got everything ready in case they had to replace it in a hurry, and the tension rose almost unbearably. Dr Craig deflated the balloon that kept the tube in position, took a deep breath, and gently eased out the curved tube. Jean felt that she herself was stifling during the few tense moments while they waited to see if the baby was going to breathe normally. Then, as they watched, his little chest moved, the lungs filled, and the baby made a noise, first a little wheezy gurgle, then a weak but unmistakable cry. The sound had an extraordinary effect on the people who had been working so hard to save him. The nurse, overcome with emotion, burst into tears, and Jean, too, felt her tears welling up. The men were moved also; Dr Craig's voice cracked as he told Jean that she had undoubtedly saved the baby's life, and even the stoic Peter later admitted to feeling an unusual prickling in his eyes when he heard the sound of a new baby coming to life inside the theatre.

Cathie had lost a lot of blood, but she was getting transfusions in both arms and Peter felt that things were finally coming back under control.

Half an hour later, Jean went out to find Douglas, who was pacing up and down outside the theatre, his face grey with worry. She sat him down, and flopped into the chair beside him.

First she told him that everything seemed to be going well, that he was now the father of an eight-pound boy, but when she explained about the baby being strangled by the umbilical cord, and Cathie's haemorrhage, she thought he was going to faint.

'How did it get around his neck like that?' he asked after he had taken a few moments to collect himself. 'I've never heard of such a thing.'

'It probably happened when they were trying to turn the baby,' replied Jean. 'Anyway, Peter did a really wonderful job in there. They should be out soon, but I wouldn't be surprised if Cathie has to stay in the hospital for a few extra days.'

Then, feeling completely exhausted, Jean dragged herself out to the car park, got into her car and drove home, hoping that the girls had gone ahead and prepared the dinner.

Chapter Sixteen

What really got up Chief Inspector Bob McLeod's nose was a telephone call that morning from a Mr Archibald Mackenzie-Forbes at the Scottish Office in Edinburgh.

'The Secretary is most distressed by the lack of progress in the case of, ah, Mrs Moira Dalgleish-Glashan,' he said, in a high-pitched English public-school voice that instantly set Bob's teeth on edge. He visualized one of those arrogant, chinless, vapid members of the ruling class, the kind who made it into society pages of the *Scotsman*, dancing at a formal Edinburgh ball, resplendent in kilt and sporran. 'And he further requests that the Dalgleish family be spared any further, ah, annoyance by your men.'

Bob took a deep breath. 'Sir,' he said, his brogue rasping like a file, 'do you not know that this is a *murder* investigation, and that the relatives of the murdered woman have to be interviewed just like everybody else?'

'I am fully aware of the facts,' said the voice. 'And I, ah, further assume that any searches and interrogations you people would normally make have been completed at Dalgleish House. What we are requesting is that from now on you keep away from the family and the house, unless it is an emergency. Is that, ah, understood?'

'I'm writing all this down, sir,' said Bob grimly. 'You

want us to treat the Dalgleishes differently from other
people involved in the murder investigation. Is that
correct, sir? You want us to change our methods of
enquiry in order not to disturb the Dalgleish family, is
that correct, sir?' Bob's voice was loud, and he was
fairly swelling with rage.

There was a silence at the other end. 'Chief
Inspector,' said Archibald McKenzie-Forbes, with a
slow, petulant emphasis. 'I don't believe you have
grasped the spirit of our conversation. We certainly
don't want to interfere in any way with the course of
justice. However, ah, I must tell you now that I find
your tone unhelpful and your attitude lacking in
cooperation. This matter will be reported to your
superiors.'

Bob grinned sourly. He knew that his superintendent
and others felt much as he did about interference from
Edinburgh or London. But, still, it was no laughing
matter to attract the hostile attention of the 'high heid
yins' in the government.

'We're all doing our verra best, sir,' he said speaking
in a slow, measured tone, calculated to make the
bureaucrat think that he was dealing with a Scots yokel
from whom not much could be expected. 'And we're
hoping that the case will be resolved shortly.'

'The Secretary certainly hopes so, too,' was the curt
reply. 'We expect to hear of an arrest in the very near
future.'

Bob waited until Archibald McKenzie-Forbes hung
up, then slammed his phone back into its cradle. At that
moment, Constable Jamieson knocked and came into
his office.

'Those people are worse than the Sassenachs,' Bob
roared. 'They're like the Vichy Government in France.'

'Yes, sir,' said Jamieson, not having the faintest idea
what Bob was talking about. Anyway, he'd come with
information for the Chief Inspector and was not to be
put off. 'Sir, Inspector Niven has had his baby, but

they're both of them nae well, I mean all three of them, counting the baby.'

'What happened?' asked Bob, his fury evaporating. 'Is Cathie all right?'

'I'm no sure, sir.' Jamieson explained that Doug had called him from the hospital to say he wouldn't be in for a while because there had been complications with Cathie and the baby.

Bob reached for the phone. Everybody knew Cathie, and she was well liked in the department. He didn't phone the hospital, but instead called home to report the news to Joy, his wife. She would alert the other wives, and would also find out what was happening to Cathie with a great deal more speed and efficiency than he could.

In the excitement, Bob forgot to pass on the message from Archibald McKenzie-Forbes to Constable Jamieson, who went back to Doug's office, which he liked to use when he knew his boss wouldn't be there. The phone was ringing, and without hesitation Jamieson picked it up. It was a young woman, from the sound of her voice, who very reluctantly identified herself as Sandra Cowie. She wanted to speak to the person in charge of the murder of Moira Dalgleish.

'You're speaking to him,' said Jamieson rather grandly. After all, he told himself, Inspector Niven was out of the running, even if temporarily, and that did leave him in charge. Also, if he told Sandra that the Inspector was unavailable, an important lead might be lost.

'You have to promise to keep my name out of it,' said Sandra.

'Certainly,' said Jamieson, feeling like a Senior Detective Inspector. 'Now kindly tell me the burden of your message.'

There was a brief silence.

'Tell you the what?'

'What you called about,' said Jamieson.

'Moira Dalgleish had a boyfriend,' said Sandra, sounding rather breathless. 'He lives next door to me, and she used to go there, even late at night, sometimes.'

'How did you know it was her?' asked Jamieson.

'Everybody knew her,' said Sandra. 'She drove around in a yellow Fiat. It was always her car outside his house.'

'Your name and address, please, ma'am,' said Jamieson, suppressing a sigh. He took a pencil from the front of Doug's desk drawer.

'I've already told you my name,' she said, but he made her repeat it. Her address, she went on, was 44 Blair Crescent. The man she was talking about lived at number 42, and he wasn't home now. He didn't come home until about six o'clock, usually.

'And his name?'

'Armand Thierry,' replied Sandra.

'You're going to have to spell that for me,' said Jamieson, although he remembered hearing it somewhere. A foreign name like that made a man automatically suspect. In the mystery books Jamieson read so avidly, a foreign name was an almost automatic tip-off, and he was still looking forward to the final episode when Monsieur Poirot would be finally unmasked.

'I'll be over shortly,' Jamieson promised. 'Until then, don't answer the door or the telephone. I'll knock on the door twice, like this,' he tapped on the telephone, 'so you'll know it's me.'

Jamieson sat down at Doug's desk, thinking perhaps he had been premature in promising to go over to the woman's house. After all, it was pretty well known that Moira Dalgleish slept around, so it would likely turn out to be just another wild-goose chase.

He decided to call the woman back and tell her to come and make a statement at police headquarters, but he'd forgotten to get her telephone number and had told her not to answer the phone, anyway. Reluctantly, he locked the door behind him and went down to his car, wishing there was somebody else he could send to talk to Sandra Cowie. After all, Douglas would certainly have sent *him*.

Rory and Bella McDermott had not been getting along well since their interviews with Douglas Niven. Rory had been fired after a polite but indignant call from the Japanese Trade Organization in Glasgow; the business-man he'd almost run over at the warehouse had complained, and the contract they had been negotiating was in peril. When he got his pink slip, Rory, who was already in a highly nervous state, grabbed his boss by the neck and had to be pulled off him by two fellow workers.

Now, Bella dreaded coming home and was thinking seriously about leaving. A couple of days after the interviews, she had woken up in the middle of the night to find Rory sitting up, staring down at her with an expression that she found terrifying.

'What's the matter with you?' she had asked.

'You know what's the matter,' he replied in a thick voice, but he wouldn't say another word. He went back to sleep, but she lay awake, motionless so as not to disturb him, until morning.

And, of course, Bella *did* know. Even now that the woman was dead, he still loved her so obsessively that he couldn't get her off his mind.

You kill the one you love. But it's better to kill the one you hate, thought Bella. That makes a lot more sense, and it was the kind of code she lived by.

Bella's friend, Audrey, who worked in a hotel in Aviemore, told her she could come and stay with her for as long as she wanted.

'You'd better get out of there,' she said when Bella told her what had been happening. 'You don't want to get found in the river, too.'

Bella didn't really worry about that, but she did feel in some danger, although she was pretty sure she still loved Rory. He seemed so unstable, and he was worse since he'd lost his job. They didn't have much money now, but he always seemed to have enough to go drinking, and when he wasn't sitting staring at her in the kitchen, he'd go for walks by himself and not come home until very late.

Maybe she should just leave for a week or two, she thought, and let things quieten down.

Late that evening, somebody drove up and dropped Rory off outside the house, and from the kitchen window Bella watched him head for the door in a stumbling but purposeful way that frightened her. She knew he was drunk, and considered locking the door and letting him find some other place to sleep, but before she had time to do it he was already inside the house.

'Bella!' His voice was rough, loud, and for some reason sounded as if he'd been rehearsing what he was going to say to her. The door slammed with a crash that shook the little house. Bella had never been really scared of him before, but there was something menacing in his voice that she hadn't heard before, and as an act of instinctive self-defence she picked up a long kitchen knife from the counter before going to the door.

'You'd better go to bed,' she said, surveying him; one hand on her hips the other behind her back, trying to establish an authority over him.

He stared back at her, and started to come forward. Instantly she brought the knife into view, and he stopped in his tracks, measuring the distance between them.

'Don't even think of it,' she said, 'if you don't want this knife in your guts.' She managed to make her voice sound firm, but she was more frightened than she'd ever been in her life.

For about a minute he cursed and yelled at her,

watching for an opening, hoping her concentration would waver for an instant. But Bella was sober, and scared for her life. Her eyes never left him and she kept the knife in front of her, where he could see it.

Finally, he moved sideways and went stumbling up the narrow stairs. At the top, he turned. 'You have to sleep sometime,' he said, and the hatred in his voice appalled her. 'I'll get you then.'

Ten minutes later, she heard the sound of snoring and, after waiting a few more minutes, she went quietly up the stairs, still holding her knife. The light was on in the bedroom, and he was slumped on top of the bed, fully dressed. Afraid that he might be pretending to sleep, she watched him for several more minutes, then stood on a chair and got her suitcase from the top of the wardrobe, turning every few moments to check that he had not moved, then, still holding the knife, she emptied her clothes from the drawers into the big old suitcase, working as fast and as silently as she could.

She never heard him coming.

'Gotcha!' She heard his triumphant grunt at the same time she felt his hands around her neck. Bella twisted around, kicked wildly back at him, but his fingers only tightened harder. She could feel the tissues of her throat beginning to cave in, and as her oxygen supply was shut off the bare bedroom-lightbulb started to go around in spirals, then become brown and dim. Knowing that she was about to die, Bella summoned her last ounce of strength, spun round and plunged the knife into Rory's chest. He gasped, released her and clutched the knife's handle, looking at her as if she were a demon from another world. As he pulled out the knife, a gush of blood and air bubbles followed the blade out of the wound. Terrified, Rory put his hand over the gash, and he began to choke as his lungs filled with blood. He fell back on the bed. Resisting an urge to let him just lie there and bleed and bubble his life away, Bella, still weak, her breath rasping painfully in her throat, stumbled downstairs and dialled 999, hoping the call would be recorded but that nobody would answer.

Chapter Seventeen

Dr Emil Patel, the psychiatrist from the Abbotsford Clinic, arrived at Dalgleish House at about one o'clock in the afternoon. He was short, dark-skinned, with thick, glossy, almost blue-black hair swept back in a bouffant style. It was his habit when making this kind of visit to take a look around the back of the house before driving up to the front entrance. Here, unfortunately, the signs were clear: the weeds in the drive, the rusty gates, the long kitchen garden wall where great gaps in the harling exposed the old red bricks, the peeling paintwork around the otherwise impressive front entrance.

After driving all the way round to the front, Dr Patel got out of his car, gave the façade of the house a professional once-over and sighed. In his experience, impoverished nobility were the worst kind of patients to deal with; they were without exception painfully stingy, complained about every fee, and tried to get out of paying their bills while at the same time looking down their aristocratic noses at him.

A woman, who looked like a cook rather than a maid, opened the door for him, and he was ushered into the vast entrance hall, so large and ill-lit that he half-expected bats to come flying out of the door.

'Mr Alastair and the others will be down in a

moment, sir,' she said. 'Please take a seat.'

Patel looked around while his eyes grew accustomed to the gloom. There was a slight but pervasive odour of old-fashioned furniture wax that reminded him of his childhood in Lahore; huge, ancient pieces of furniture; a round inlaid pedestal table; faded, overstuffed chairs with sturdy square legs too crudely crafted to be French or even English; high, glass-fronted bookcases that looked as if they had never been opened, and a big, oak refectory table at the far end, with a few magazines and a modern plastic globe on it.

A door opened and a youngish man walked in, well-dressed, with tanned, good looks and the take-charge air of someone who is used to being in command. Even before he came up to introduce himself, Dr Patel guessed that this was Alastair Dalgleish, MP for the Southern Scottish counties.

'I hope you found your way without too much trouble,' he said. 'I saw your car coming round the back.'

'In error I took the service entrance,' replied Dr Patel in a courteous, sing-song voice. 'Your own instructions were impeccable.'

'As I explained to you several days ago,' said Alastair, 'my brother's condition is deteriorating, and his wife and I wish to have your professional opinion. You come very well recommended.'

'May I ask who . . .?' said Dr Patel delicately, but Alastair ignored the interruption.

'Colin is in the upstairs day-room,' he said, 'if you would care to follow me.'

Colin was on a couch, and seemed to be particularly upset. Elspeth and Patricia were sitting on chairs opposite the couch, trying to comfort him.

Colin looked up with an aggrieved expression. 'I'm glad you've come,' he said to Dr Patel. 'They're trying to poison me.'

Dr Patel sat down, well aware that paranoid people

were occasionally correct about their fears. He smiled and nodded at the two ladies.

'Who do you think is poisoning you, Sir Colin?'

'My teacher,' he said, staring at Dr Patel with eyes full of tears. 'Miss Duff. She's always hated me. She puts it into my medicine.'

Dr Patel looked at Alastair.

'Miss Duff was his teacher when he first went to school,' he said. 'I was in her class two years later. She's been dead for about ten years.'

Dr Patel nodded, and pulled his chair up close to the couch.

'Sir Colin,' he said, very gently, 'I would like to ask you a few questions. Do you know what day it is today?'

'Thursday, I suppose.' A tear trickled down his cheek. 'That was the day Moira was killed, wasn't it, Alastair?'

'Quite possibly, old chap,' replied Alastair. He turned to Dr Patel. 'He seems to have become a lot worse since that tragedy.'

Colin curled up on the couch in a foetal position and refused to say anything more.

'Sir Colin,' said Dr Patel after several attempts to communicate with him, 'I think it would be best if you came to spend a few days with us at the Abbotsford Clinic. I think we can make you feel a great deal better.'

Colin, his face firmly pressed against the back of the couch, said nothing. Dr Patel got up and motioned the others to come outside with him.

'I'm afraid Sir Colin's in a seriously withdrawn state,' he said. 'He had the classical signs of schizophrenia, with delusions and paranoia. Has he been taking any medicine of any kind?'

'Imipramine,' said Elspeth. 'That was prescribed by Dr Waltham Baker in Harley Street. You probably know of him.'

Dr Patel nodded.

'He also gets a multi-vitamin preparation.' Elspeth

was wringing her hands, obviously distressed. 'It seems to help him, too, although not so much recently.' She had brought the bottles down to show Dr Patel, and he checked the labels.

'We'll probably give him some different medication,' he said, 'but, of course, we'll have to do a complete evaluation first. Now . . .' Dr Patel turned to Alastair, apparently the only fiscally responsible man there, and approached the most important topic with his usual delicacy. 'Mr Dalgleish, let's talk for a moment about the financial arrangements concerning Sir Colin's stay at the Abbotsford Clinic . . .'

'He's not going,' said Elspeth.

They all looked at her in astonishment. 'Elspeth,' Alastair was the first to speak, 'I thought we'd decided over a week ago that—'

'That was then,' said Elspeth, her voice trembling but firm. 'I've changed my mind. If Colin needs treatment he can get it here.'

'That's perfectly all right, madam,' said Dr Patel courteously. He turned to Alastair. 'There was another matter you wished to discuss, was there not, sir?'

Alastair shifted his feet and glanced at Elspeth. 'Yes. The problem of legal responsibilities for my brother's affairs.'

'Perhaps we could talk about that in another room,' said Dr Patel, his voice as professionally discreet as an undertaker's.

Jamieson stopped the car outside Sandra Cowie's house, and was about to get out when he remembered that on this type of visit Doug always left his car further down the street, next to a shop or a vacant lot, because people didn't like to have a police car parked outside their homes. So, watched by curious eyes from the neighbouring houses, Jamieson drove a little further down Blair Crescent, parked and walked back to number 44.

Sandra was a small, pretty, bird-like woman, somewhere in her mid-thirties. Like everybody else, she had seen the car stop outside her house then move on, and she wasn't amused, but her annoyance vanished when Jamieson came up the short path to her front door.

'My, you *are* a hunk, aren't you?' she said admiringly. 'Do come in.'

Jamieson coughed to cover his embarrassment. 'This is a really big house,' he said, looking around at the big windows, the piano and the pleasant furniture. 'Do you live here all by yourself?'

'Ever since my divorce,' she said, eyeing Jamieson hungrily.

'Well, now, Mrs Cowie . . .' Jamieson sat down in an easy chair and took a pen from his breast pocket.

'I prefer Ms, if you don't mind,' said Sandra demurely. 'Mrs makes people think of an old married woman, don't you think? Anyway, you could just call me Sandra, if you like.'

Jamieson barely heard her, immersed as he was in organizing the sequence of his questions. 'You mentioned that the deceased was in the habit of visiting your next-door neighbour in the dead of night?'

'Well, it wasn't *always* the dead of night. Sometimes it was during the day — at weekends — but, yes sometimes she came by night.' Sandra made it sound very mysterious.

'Tell me a wee bit about your neighbour, Mrs Cowie.'

'Ms. His name is Armand Thierry,' she said, looking through the window as if he might be lurking in the bushes outside. 'He's quiet, but not exactly sociable, if you see what I mean. He has a beauty salon on South Street. I went there once, you know, just to see what it was like.'

Jamieson shifted in his chair, and Sandra took the hint.

'All right, he's about five-foot-ten, slender, with a

small sandy moustache. His skin is shiny, sort of tight-looking, and he always wears sandals.'

'Even in winter?' asked Jamieson, incredulously.

'Not in winter, of course not.' Sandra laughed up at him from a low ottoman upon which she had installed herself. 'Except in his house. Why on earth would he wear sandals outside?'

Jamieson felt the beginnings of a headache, a faint throbbing between his temples.

'What else do you know about him?' he asked. Sandra was really quite nice-looking, he realized. She had a smooth complexion, bright eyes, small white teeth and a quick smile. Jamieson liked petite women, maybe because of the way they had to look up at him, but on the other hand he often felt clumsy and ox-like in their presence.

'Nothing. Nobody does. He's not married. When he first came. I ... well ... I asked round, and, of course, spoke to him, asked where he was from, that kind of thing.'

'So?' Jamieson had the impression that Sandra had tried to strike up a relationship with her new neighbour but hadn't had much success.

'Well, a person likes to know where their neighbours are from,' replied Sandra, a little on the defensive. 'Wouldn't you?'

Jamieson thought about it. 'I know where mine come from,' he said. 'There's Dod Meldrum on one side, born and bred here in Perth, and the same goes for old Mrs Fergus, on the other side.'

A brief silence followed.

'She never stayed very long,' said Sandra.

Jamieson, thinking about Mrs Fergus and the hip replacement she was supposed to have soon, stared at Sandra.

'Moira,' she prompted. 'At Mr Thierry's house. Maybe half an hour, sometimes twenty minutes. Just long enough, I suppose, to do whatever they were doing.' A faint blush spread over Sandra's face and neck.

Embarrassed, Jamieson put his head down and wrote.

'Aye,' he said. 'Anything else about him that you can think of?'

Sandra considered, but she was having trouble concentrating, and her eyes kept wandering over Jamieson's big, muscular body. 'There are a lot of little scars on his face,' she said finally, tilting up her own flawless chin and running her finger along the side of her jaw. 'Around here and on his neck. Maybe he was in an accident,' she suggested. Again there was a silence while Jamieson transferred the information into his notebook. Sandra watched him as he wrote.

'Do you know if Mr Thierry has any other friends? Does he entertain?'

'I don't know, but I don't think so, not much anyway. Last summer he had the people who work for him over for a barbecue in his garden, but it rained.' Sandra's smirk of satisfaction told Jamieson that she hadn't been invited.

'Well, that's about all, Ms Cowie,' he said, closing his notebook. 'Unless there's anything else you haven't mentioned.'

Sandra took a deep breath. 'Do you have a first name, Constable Jamieson?'

'Not while I'm on duty, ma'am,' he replied sternly.

'Do you ever go dancing?' she persisted.

He stood up and smiled at her upturned face. 'Sandra, I'm no' allowed to fraternize while I'm on a job, but I can tell you that on Saturday evenings I sometimes go down to Electric Whispers on Canal Street.'

On the way back to headquarters, Jamieson tried to keep his mind on Armand Thierry, but Sandra's cute little face kept on intruding on his thoughts. He liked her; she was older than him, and he liked that too. Older women were usually more sensible, he'd found, more down to earth, didn't make the sort of demands that the younger girls made, and best of all they were past the giggling stage. If there was one thing Jamieson hated, it was a giggler.

Armand Thierry. Jamieson remembered the name; Elspeth Dalgleish had mentioned it. He knew where Thierry's beauty parlour was, but had never been there. On the spur of the moment, he decided to stop in and ask Thierry about Moira Dalgleish.

Everybody looked up as he entered. It wasn't just Jamieson's size; there was something about him, the ponderous way he walked and held himself, that always attracted attention.

Armand's insides did a somersault when Jamieson introduced himself, but he kept enough *sang-froid* to lead him back into his tiny office.

'And so what can I do for you, *monsieur*?'

'What do you know about Moira Dalgleish?' asked Jamieson bluntly. He looked around the office; the walls were covered with framed posters of men and women modelling different haircuts, and the desk was covered with jars of face cream, nail varnish and other beauty products.

Armand thought his heart had stopped beating when he heard the question, but he managed to say, 'Yes, a very sad tragedy. A fine young woman like that, to drown in the river.'

'She was *found* in the river,' replied Jamieson, looking hard at Armand. 'That doesn't mean she was drowned.'

Armand licked his lips. 'I am deeply distressed by this tragedy,' he said. 'I knew Miss Moira, and even from time to time employed her as a consultant on beauty matters.'

'Did she go to your house?' asked Jamieson. He noticed that Armand was pale and his hands were shaking, and Jamieson wondered briefly if he had a drinking problem.

'Yes. Sometimes it . . . wasn't convenient for her to come to the salon,' said Armand.

A grin spread slowly across Jamieson's face. That explained it. Sandra had evidently thought Moira's visits were of a more personal nature, when in fact they had merely been talking business.

'Well, we needed to check up in that, Mr Thierry, thank you,' said Jamieson. 'Is there anything you can think of that might help us in our investigation?'

Armand, not trusting himself to speak, shook his head.

Jamieson turned to the door. 'Thanks again, then, Mr Thierry. Sorry to have troubled you.'

Armand could feel his legs trembling as he ushered the constable out.

Jamieson got back into his car, sat back in the seat and exhaled a lungful of air. That had been a close call: if he hadn't personally stopped in to see Mr Thierry, he would have put all that nonsense Sandra had told him about Thierry and Moira in his report.

He fastened his seat-belt, checked his mirror and pulled away from the kerb. Sandra had made an honest mistake, he was sure of it, and Jamieson shrugged expansively to himself. Women always looked for romantic angles to every situation, so one couldn't really blame them when they turned out to be wrong. Anyway, not all had been lost; he might be seeing Sandra on Saturday night. He felt pretty sure that she'd appear at Electric Whispers at some time during the evening.

Chapter Eighteen

For a while, Doug's anxiety about Cathie and his new son had put everything else out of his mind, but now that Dr McIntosh had pronounced both of them out of danger, he was concerned about what Jamieson might be doing on his own. Cathie, exhausted and sore, but now back in her hospital bed, could see his restlessness.

'Awa' you go, Douggie,' she said, letting go of his hand. 'Anyway, I need to sleep now. You'll find a phone in the hall outside the ward.'

Doug didn't argue. On the way out he met Fiona Montrose coming in. She looked anxious and upset, and grabbed him by the arm. 'How is she?' she asked. 'And the baby? Mum told me what happened.'

Doug reported that they were both improving, and Fiona gave him a quick hug before hurrying in to see Cathie. Right behind Fiona came a boy carrying a huge bouquet of pink and yellow roses. 'I'm looking for a Mrs Niven,' he said.

'I'll show you where she is,' said Doug. The card that came with the roses had the signatures of Bob McLeod and several of his colleagues. Cathie wept, as much from tiredness as from emotion, and when Doug left the ward again, Fiona was holding Cathie's hand and talking to her, trying to make her laugh with stories from her work.

Doug arrived at his office at the same time as Bob

McLeod, who was puffing hard on his pipe and wearing a leather-trimmed, knitted police jacket, which he'd bought in the States.

'Glad you're back, Doug,' he said. 'I got a phone call from some twit at the Scottish Office in Edinburgh. Apparently the Secretary of State for Scotland, no less, wants us to ease off on the Dalgleishes. We're not to bother them any more, OK?'

'What do they care?' asked Douglas, surprised. He opened the door. Jamieson was sitting at Doug's desk, dozing. He jumped up when they came in, knocking the chair over in his panic.

'Out,' said Douglas. Jamieson picked up his jacket and left, embarrassed but trying to look dignified.

'Come back in ten minutes,' Doug called after him. He turned to Bob, who had installed himself in the hot seat, 'Why are we getting attention from such a high altitude?'

Bob shrugged, puffed on his pipe, and in an instant the small office was filled with blue smoke. Doug coughed.

'It must have something to do with Alastair Dalgleish,' said Bob. 'As an MP, he has the clout. Certainly none of the others do.' His lip curled at the thought of the ineffectual Sir Colin.

'What do you know about him?' asked Doug. 'I mean Alastair. He seemed OK when I interviewed him.'

Bob shrugged. 'He's had his ups and downs. A friend of mine in Whitehall told me that Alastair was involved in some kind of scandal there — but you know how it is: when you're senior enough, it gets hushed up — then he went into politics.'

'What kind of scandal? A woman?' asked Doug. 'Or a man?' he added quickly to show that he was thoroughly sophisticated in such matters.

'No idea. It might be worth finding out, though.'

The phone rang, and Douglas picked it up. It was the hospital, and Douglas's heart almost stopped. But it had nothing to do with Cathie. A man had been picked up after a 999 call, almost dead from a stab wound in the chest. He was in the operating theatre, and the word was that the lung had been punctured but otherwise his injuries were relatively minor. The victim's name was Rory McDermott. He'd fallen on a knife, according to his wife, but the woman could hardly speak, and had the worst bruises on her neck the ambulance men had ever seen.

'He was drunk,' croaked Bella. She had wrapped a tartan scarf around her neck. 'It was an accident.'

'The neighbours can't understand it,' said Douglas in a concerned tone. 'Do you mind if we sit down?' He didn't wait for permission, and pointed to a chair for Jamieson. 'They say the two of you were always like a pair of love-birds.'

Bella snorted, then coughed.

'Until Rory started up with that Moira Dalgleish,' said Jamieson.

'*She* started up with *him*,' said Bella, but her voice gave out, and she put a hand up to her neck.

'Then she dropped him, right?' asked Doug.

Bella shrugged.

'And he was very upset about it?' Doug watched her carefully. She nodded.

'He became obsessed about her?' Doug went on.

Bella sat very still and said nothing, staring at the wall behind Doug.

'Obsessed enough to kill her when she wouldn't come back to him, do you think?'

Bella pursed her lips and shook her head briefly, but there was no force behind her denial. She raised her hands and massaged the back of her neck.

'I think you should see a doctor,' said Douglas. 'We can give you a lift down to Dr Montrose's office, if you like.'

'No,' said Bella emphatically. 'I can take the bus if I want to go.'

'Did he ever hurt you like this before?'

Tears appeared in Bella's eyes, but she didn't say anything.

'Do you want to press charges?' asked Doug. 'You'd be entirely within your rights.'

'He didn't do nothing,' said Bella. 'It was an accident.'

Doug asked a few more questions, but it was clear that he was getting nowhere. Bella might be scared enough to leave Rory, but she would never turn him in.

Douglas stood up, and Jamieson followed suit.

'You know where to reach us if you want to tell us anything,' said Doug.

Bella opened the door and slammed it behind them, mainly for the benefit of the neighbours.

Douglas pulled away from the kerb with a squeal of tyres. 'We're going to the hospital,' he said. 'You go and check on Rory, see what sort of shape he's in, talk to him if you can. I'm going upstairs to spend a couple of minutes with Cathie.'

'Do you think Rory did it, sir?' asked Jamieson, more to take his mind of the way Doug was driving than for information.

'Fit the pieces together for me,' answered Doug, swerving to avoid a lorry that was slowing down to make a right turn. There was still snow on the side of the road and the car slid for a dozen or so yards before Doug regained control and drove on. 'First, do we have a motive?' he continued as if nothing had happened.

Jamieson's eyes were shut tight. He took a deep breath. 'Well,' he said, 'it could be jealousy, sir.'

'Right. Put yourself in his shoes, Jamieson. Here he is, desperately in love with a woman who's out of his class, he dreams of marrying her, becoming a gentleman of leisure. Then she drops him, hard. He can't sleep for thinking about her, he's obsessed, then he hears she's going with somebody else, or a lot of other men, who knows, and he gets her to see him one last time, then in a fit of rage, or as a premeditated murder, he strangles the woman and dumps her body in the river.'

Jamieson opened his eyes a crack, and shut them again when he saw a van rapidly approaching them in the same lane. Douglas was overtaking a car, and was on the wrong side of the road.

'We know he's a violent man,' went on Douglas. 'He's had three previous arrests for disorderly behaviour of one kind or another. Not what else do we have?'

'He tried to strangle his wife.'

'And it was a close thing, from the looks of her,' said Doug. 'But, of course, if she doesn't charge him we don't have anything to go on.'

'Yes, sir,' said Jamieson, gritting his teeth as he was slammed against the seat-belt restraints, 'but isn't all that circumstantial? Whereas the lure we found on her would be real evidence, in court, I mean, isn't that right, sir?'

Doug glanced at Jamieson in surprise. 'Have you been reading for your sergeant's exam, Jamieson?'

'Yes, sir.'

'You're quite right. And the lure's the only piece of real evidence we have, so the circumstantial evidence would have to be pretty good to stand up in court. We need something more, I'm thinking. We'll get no help from Bella. Maybe the staff up at Dalgleish House saw something on the night Moira disappeared.'

'I spoke to Emily,' said Jamieson. 'She said she didn't see nothing.'

'Anything,' corrected Douglas.

'I was quoting *verbatim*, sir,' said Jamieson indignantly. 'Those were the actual words she used. And Kevin Marshall and Maggie were away at the time, and that's it.'

Douglas pulled up outside the main hospital entrance, and Jamieson heaved a sigh of relief, thankful that he had completed the journey in one piece.

'I'll pick you up in an hour's time,' said Doug.

'I can make my own way back, thank you, sir,' said Jamieson hastily. 'It's a fine day for a walk.'

Chapter Nineteen

The day after the eventful birth of Douglas Niven Jr, there was a pause in the action at the surgery, and Jean closed the door to her office and sat down to think about the things that were disturbing her more and more about Moira Dalgleish's murder.

Jean's strong maternal instincts made her worry first about Moira's little orphaned son. A chill passed through her for a moment, and she picked up the phone to call Elspeth Dalgleish.

'I just wanted to be sure the baby's all right,' she told her.

'He's fine,' replied Elspeth. Her voice was listless. 'He's with some cousins near Edinburgh, and now they say they want to adopt him, which is the best solution all round, I suppose.' Her voice faded, and Jean could almost feel her anxiety and despondency. 'Jean, I'm glad you phoned, because we didn't finish our conversation the other day. And I want to talk to you about Colin. At this point, he's not even able—'

'I'll come out to see him,' interrupted Jean, a thought coming into her head. 'This afternoon, after my surgery. All right? Then we'll be able to finish our chat.'

'Thank you, that would be wonderful, Jean. Would you like to stay for dinner?'

'I don't think so, Elspeth, thanks all the same. I have

my family to feed. I'll see you at about four-thirty, then.'

Jean put down the phone, fighting a growing feeling of disquiet. She thought for a moment then, after dialling directory inquiries, phoned a number in London. The young man who answered was very helpful, but didn't have the information she needed, and promised to look it up. Jean said she'd call back next day.

At lunchtime, Jean stopped at the hospital to see Cathie, and was surprised to see Fiona chatting with Cathie. She had obviously been there for some time, and looked a little embarrassed when Jean came in.

'I took a day off, Mum,' she explained. 'They owe me. And I was anxious about Cathie and the baby, so—'

'That's fine, Fiona,' Jean interrupted. 'I'm really glad that the two of you are friends again.'

Cathie, still looking very pale and tired, smiled and squeezed Fiona's hand. 'She's a fine quine, your daughter. I hope my son grows up to be as good a person as her.'

'How's he doing?' asked Jean. 'I mean Douglas Junior.' The last report she'd had from the nursery was encouraging.

'Better. He still makes a noise like a steam engine when he breathes, but . . .' Cathie smiled, 'as long as he *is* breathing, I don't care how much noise he makes!'

'He's beautiful,' said Fiona, smiling. 'Just beautiful.'

Jean went over to refill Cathie's water glass at the sink.

'I'll see you at home for dinner, then, Fiona,' she said.

'No, I'm staying here,' she replied. 'The nurse said she'd give me a meal with the other patients.'

'Don't think she's here just to keep you company,' said Jean to Cathie. 'It's the hospital food she's really interested in.'

'What are you making tonight, Mum?' retorted Fiona, 'The frozen fish casserole?'

'Well, your father likes it, even if you girls don't,' said Jean, getting up to go. 'Actually, we're having salmon steaks one of my patients brought in, so there.'

'Keep me one, *please*!' Fiona called out as Jean went off to take a look at baby Douglas.

Later, as she drove back to the surgery, Jean started to think again about Moira Dalgleish and the various people who had hovered around her, one of whom had taken the desperate step of killing her.

Why? Jean knew of several pieces that didn't fit; several statements that people connected with Moira had made that had turned out to be untrue; but telling lies certainly wasn't the same thing as strangling a person, and they might not even be related. The thing that stumped Jean most of all was the apparent lack of a motive. And then something Alastair had said came into her mind, and Jean's heart sank. If it was true, then it would change the whole complexion of the case.

Jean forced herself to return to the initial question she had posed. Why? What did anyone have to gain from her death? Certainly it wasn't wealth or position; there was nothing of any major value to inherit from her, no title, no wealth. Could it have been her poor dotty father, in a fit of pathological anger? It seemed unlikely; when something upset him, Sir Colin would be more likely to dissolve into tears than go and strangle someone.

Elspeth? There didn't appear to be any motive there either. She seemed scared about her own safety, but, of course, that could be a cover.

Alastair? Jean shrugged with frustration. He seemed a nice enough person, was as distinguished a politician as politicians could be. As far as she could tell, he was comfortably off, and in the running to become the leader of the up-and-coming Scottish Popular Party. If what people were saying was true, he might indeed become the first Prime Minister of Scotland. So what possible motive could he have for killing his niece?

Patricia, his wife, was less of a known quantity. Douglas had discovered that she was his second wife, came from a well-known Edinburgh family and was generally thought of as more ornamental than functional, and from the little Jean had seen of her, it seemed a correct enough evaluation. But, when she thought about everything she knew about the situation, Jean realized that Patricia might well have a motive, and a very powerful one at that.

The only other person who would legitimately have been in the house that night was Emily, the cook, and she seemed such an unlikely suspect that Jean took her off the list.

She sighed. Inevitably, the whole case seemed to be coming around to Rory and Bella McDermott, with Armand Thierry hovering in the wings somewhere. But right now, Jean knew that Rory was Doug's prime suspect. He was a former lover of Moira's, hadn't got over her emotionally, and, of course, his fishing lure had been found on her body. Douglas considered this to be symbolic, that the lure and hook had been placed there to show that he'd finally caught her, if only in death, but Jean didn't think Rory would be particuarly interested in symbolism, especially if it could lead to his arrest. But the circumstantial evidence was certainly strong, maybe sufficient for Douglas to arrest him. Pressure was being applied to the Tayside Police from the Scottish Office, and it would suit a lot of people if Rory turned out to be the killer. But why had he attacked Bella? Had the death of Moira made him insane? Had he already been driven mad and killed Moira?

And how about Bella? She was a quiet, unnoticeable woman, who had lived peaceably with Rory for several years. What had happened that night? What domestic crisis could have occurred that contained such fury that they both tried to kill each other? Maybe she had nagged him too much about Moira, because, of course, she must have known about his infatuation with her. The different possibilities were starting to dance alarmingly inside Jean's head, when a thought struck her with such force that she almost drove straight through a red light on South Street. Maybe Rory had tried to strangle Bella because *she* had killed Moira.

Douglas met Jamieson back at his office.

'Well, lad, what did Rory tell you?' he asked, more relaxed after finding both Cathie and Douglas Junior in good health.

'Nothing,' replied Jamieson simply. 'I asked him a lot of questions, but all he did was stare at me, then he called me a couple of names I don't care to repeat, sir.'

'Is he going to be in the hospital long?'

'The nurse said probably two more days. He wasn't that badly injured, on the inside, that is. Anyway, that's what she said.'

'Maybe we should put somebody up there to keep an eye on him.'

'He isn't going anywhere,' said Jamieson quickly, aware that if anybody was going to be detailed to stand watch over Rory McDermott it would be him. 'He's got an IV in his arm and, anyway, he doesn't have anywhere to escape to.'

'Make sure you check on him tomorrow,' said Doug. 'Meanwhile, you haven't brought me up to date with what you did while I was at the hospital.'

Jamieson thought. 'Nothing much, sir, after I'd gone to see that foreign chap in his shop.' Jamieson sat back and cracked his knuckles, annoyed at himself. He had decided previously not even to mention that incident.

Doug stared at him. 'What foreign chap are you referring to, may I ask?'

Jamieson scowled, trapped. He told Doug about Sandra Cowie, and his visit to Armand Thierry's beauty salon.

'That was a good piece of work, Jamieson,' said Doug. 'We know he had dealings with Moira Dalgleish, and that opens up a whole new set of possibilities.'

Jamieson shook his head. 'I'm afraid not, sir. You see, what I didn't tell you is that Mr Thierry only saw Moira Dalgleish regarding business matters.'

'And how do you happen to be so certain of that, Jamieson?' Doug's voice was taking on a tone that Jamieson knew and feared.

'Well, sir, he said . . .' Jamieson gulped, realizing how this was going to sound to Douglas. 'That's what he told me, and he seemed very honest, for a foreigner, sir, so there seemed no point in going on about it.'

'Did you do a background check on him, Jamieson? Previous occupations, where he's lived? Did you at least find out if he has a record of arrests?'

'No, sir,' replied Jamieson, sheepishly. 'There didn't seem to be any need . . .'

Doug took a deep breath. 'Jamieson, we have a lead on a man who may have had an intimate relationship with the murdered woman and you just dropped it? Because the suspect said he only had a business relationship with her?'

'I didn't think of it that way, sir, I'm sorry.' Douglas Niven always did this, tried to make a fool of him when all he was doing was exercising his judgement.

Douglas tried to keep calm. 'That's all right, Jamieson. No harm's been done. Now, the first thing I want you to do is find out all you can about this Mr Thierry, then we'll both go and have a wee chat with him.'

'Yes, sir,' said Jamieson, relieved that he'd got off so lightly, and thankful that Cathie Niven was doing so well, otherwise he'd have had an official reprimand or worse.

The information came in on the computer from Glasgow less than an hour later, and it didn't amount to much. Armand Thierry seemed to have been born only four years before; there was simply no information beyond the fact that he was domiciled in Perth, and had a National Registration Number with a code indicating it had been issued in London.

'He must have come from somewhere,' said Douglas.

'He's got a French name,' said Jamieson. 'Maybe he came from France or Belgium or one of those places.'

'Then he'd have a Euro passport number and some kind of documentation if he came here to work rather than as a tourist.' Douglas scratched the top of his head. 'This is really weird. I'll phone Jock Nairn in Immigration tomorrow. He'll be able to find out for us.'

'Maybe Interpol would know about him,' said Jamieson.

'They're only interested in big international criminals,' said Doug.

'Well, he's international,' said Jamieson, 'judging by his name, anyway.'

'I tell you what,' said Doug, 'if we can get a set of fingerprints from him, we can put that on the central computer and they can tell us if there's a match-up within an hour.'

'How are you going to get prints without arresting him?' asked Jamieson.

'Leave it to me,' said Doug.

Chapter Twenty

Alastair Dalgleish spent a day in Edinburgh talking to his constituents; he gave an after-dinner lecture to a crowded audience, then took the early morning flight to Gatwick to make an appearance in the House and another on BBC television, but he was anxious to get back to Perth. There was a lot to be done. After the psychiatrist had certified Colin as mentally incompetent, with Elspeth's consent Alastair had started on the legalities of assuming control of the estate. He had to face the huge task of sorting out the mess that Colin had left everything in. Apart from Dalgleish House, there were several sizeable land-holdings, one in particular near Dunfermline, on the edge of a new industrial estate. Colin had resisted pressure to sell it, on the grounds that it had become some kind of nature preserve, and because their tenants had farmed the arable part of the land for generations.

Alastair had already been in touch with Curry McNish, one of the largest land-developers in Scotland, and the machinery to consummate the sale of the land had already been set in motion. And when that went through, finally there would be some much-needed money available.

He was now on his way back to Perth in his grey Jaguar, accompanied by Patricia, who was asleep next to him.

'Do you think they're going to arrest that McDermott fellow?' asked Patricia, waking up as they slowed for the tollbooths at the Forth Bridge.

Alastair shrugged. 'I have no idea. There doesn't seem much doubt that he was one of Moira's emotional casualties.'

'There were certainly several of those,' agreed Patricia, who then closed her eyes again and said no more.

Jean checked her black bag to make sure she'd packed all the diagnostic instruments she would need, then phoned Lisbie at work to tell her she'd be late. Lisbie said she'd make dinner.

'I don't suppose Fiona will be home, do you think, Mum?' she asked.

Fiona had been spending most of her spare time with Cathie at the hospital, and had reportedly fallen in love with the baby.

'Make enough for her,' said Jean. 'So if she does come back she won't feel excluded.' The roads were clear now, except for a few sheltered roadside patches of snow, where long grass-stems stuck above the surface like whiskers.

Elspeth had evidently been on the lookout, because the door opened as soon as Jean pressed the old-fashioned porcelain doorbell.

She seemed more nervous than usual, and looked over Jean's shoulder as if she were expecting someone to come in after her.

'W – w – what . . .' Elspeth was stammering, 'what would you like to do first, Jean? Colin's in his room, or we could—'

'Let's go and see him first,' said Jean, and Elspeth seemed to relax a little, simply because Jean had made the decision and it was one thing less for her to worry about.

She led Jean upstairs, through the dank corridors,

where wallpaper was peeling off the walls, and stopped outside a door near the far end. She listened for a moment, her head cocked, looking, Jean thought, like a sad, frightened little bird who didn't know which way to turn.

She put her hand up, hesitated, and whispered 'Sometimes he gets very angry, but I think he's all right now.' Then she knocked and opened the door.

Colin was lying on his bed, rigid, his eyes closed, and for a moment Jean's heart almost stopped. Then he gave a hiccup and sat bolt upright. It seemed to take him a few moments to recognize Jean, but then he very politely asked her to sit down.

'This time it's not a social call, Sir Colin,' she told him, smiling. 'I'd like to examine you, if you don't mind.' Jean's tone was kindly enough, but brooked no disagreement. Obediently, Sir Colin took off his pyjama top.

'Everything, please,' said Jean, and off came the bottoms too, although Colin hesitated and glowered at Elspeth for a second. Jean's examination was very thorough. She listened to his chest, examined his cranial nerves, looked into his eyes with her ophthalmoscope. She found some slowness of his reflexes and a tremor which made her think of Parkinson's disease, but he didn't have enough other signs for her to make that diagnosis.

'What medicines is he taking?' asked Jean, putting her equipment back in her bag.

'I don't know what they're called,' stammered Elspeth. 'Wait, I'll go and get them.' She came back with two bottles, both unsealed. Jean peered at the first label, then put on her glasses and tried again. It was Librium, prescribed a year before by a physician whose address was at the better end of Harley Street. Jean shook out a couple of tablets, and recognized the shape. They were indeed Libriums. The other bottle was labelled as a liquid multi-vitamin supplement. Jean

unscrewed the lid. The bottle was full, and when Jean
sniffed it had the characteristic pungent smell of the B
vitamins. Over the top of the bottle, Jean could see
Elspeth watching her with a kind of hypnotized anxiety.

'How long has Sir Colin been taking this?' Jean
asked, screwing the top back on.

'A couple of years,' replied Elspeth. 'The same
doctor prescribed it, and he's kept on taking it, haven't
you, Colin?'

Sir Colin shrugged.

'Alastair gets them from Boots in little cases of six
bottles,' went on Elspeth, then looked uncomfortable.
'It saves going every couple of weeks, and it costs less
that way.'

Elspeth started to help Colin to get his pyjamas on, so
Jean took the two bottles back into the bathroom. The
place was rather untidy, and it took her a few moments
to find the cardboard box lying on its side by the sink.
She hesitated, put the Librium bottle on the sink and the
vitamin bottle in the pocket of her skirt, then came back
into the bedroom.

'Did Dr Patel prescribe any other medicine for him?'
she asked Elspeth.

'Not yet,' replied Elspeth. 'He said he might next time
he comes.'

Jean tried to chat with Colin, but he was barely
coherent, and his obvious anxiety made it even more
difficult for him to speak. After several minutes, Jean
got up. Colin turned away from her, faced the wall and
curled up in his bed, and the two women left, stepping
softly out of the room. Elspeth closed the door behind
her with meticulous care. 'He hates sudden noises,' she
whispered to Jean. 'They make him very angry. Now
let's go into my day room where we can talk in peace
without being interrupted.'

Jean followed her into a pleasant, airy room with big
windows and comfortable but inexpensive furniture.
Elspeth indicated a chair for Jean, then sat back in a

big armchair. Jean glanced at her watch with some ostentation; she had to get home soon and Elspeth looked as if she was settling in for the duration.

'What was Dr Patel's diagnosis on Sir Colin?' asked Jean.

'He said he probably had . . . it had two words, sounded like parachute or paramour something . . . I don't know anything about medical terms.' Elspeth's voice reflected her insecurity; it was clear that this was all a bit beyond her.

Jean thought for a moment. 'Paranoia? Paranoid schizophrenia?'

'That's it, the last one you said. Anyway he said there wasn't very much he could do with Colin as an out-patient. I think he wanted to get him into his clinic, but I wouldn't allow it.' Elspeth's face took on a stubborn expression. 'Jean, I've decided to take him to the Lange Clinic in Switzerland. It's supposed to be the best in the world for this kind of thing. I haven't told Alastair, so please don't mention it.'

Jean, who knew how much it cost to be a patient in the Lange clinic, was surprised, but said nothing. How Elspeth got the money was none of her business.

Elspeth ran out of steam; talking to Jean her voice became barely audible, and she seemed close to breaking point. Jean put a sympathetic arm around her, and Elspeth burst into tears. 'It's all too much,' she said. 'With Colin and everything. Moira was my only child,' she went on. 'She wasn't always . . . careful about who she went with, and I'm sure she overdid things, but she . . . she wasn't a bad person, and didn't deserve to be killed like that.'

'Who do you think could have done it, Elspeth?' asked Jean quietly, watching her. There was something about Elspeth's sorrow that disturbed her.

'I can't imagine,' said Elspeth, twisting a hand-kerchief in her hands.

'How did Alastair and Patricia get along with Moira?'

'Just fine,' said Elspeth quickly. 'She was Alastair's favourite niece, and they always hit it off. Until Moira went off to get married, that is, because it was all so sudden and everything. There was a bit of tension between them, but nothing, well, nothing that would lead to . . .' Elspeth put her head between her hands and sobbed.

'Tell me a bit more about Moira and her marriage,' asked Jean. 'Was he a local man?'

'It was what they call a whirlwind romance, I suppose,' said Elspeth, sounding as if she didn't believe in any kind of romance. 'She met Michael Glashan in London, at some ball. He was on his way to Hong Kong a few days later, and she decided to follow him out there.'

'Just like that?'

'Just like that. Alastair was the only family member who actually met him. They had dinner at Alastair's club, I believe, the day before he left.'

'Did Moira join them?'

'They don't allow women in the Athenaeum,' replied Elspeth.

'Oh, of course,' Jean tried to imagine what the Athenaeum was like, and had a vision of high ceilings, windows overlooking a park, black leather armchairs, ancient colonels, old carpets and quiet servants, and a funereal and unbreakable silence hanging over everything. In her mind, it was awful.

'What about Patricia? Did you know her before she married Alastair?'

Elspeth's lips compressed ever so slightly. 'No. Actually, she was a *divorcée*.' Elspeth said the word as if it were something she would rather have avoided without comment, like a cow-pat in a field.

'How did she and Moira get along?'

'Moira didn't pay much attention to Patricia, who didn't like that very much, but basically I don't think they had major disagreements. Jean,' Elspeth was looking flustered again, 'I actually want to talk to you about—'

'Just one last thing, Elspeth,' said Jean. 'How did Moira get along with your cook, Emily?'

'Not well,' said Elspeth, looking up, surprised that Jean should mention their cook. 'Emily went for her because of that Rory McDermott. You know about him, don't you?'

Jean nodded.

'Did you know they were cousins? I mean Rory and Emily? That whole family has worked for the Dalgleishes for almost a hundred years, on and off, not counting wars and things.'

Jean hid her astonishment. 'Do you think Emily might have killed Moira?' It seemed such an unlikely possibility that Jean gave a little laugh.

'Probably not,' said Elspeth. 'But she was seriously angry with Moira, even before she went off to get married, and I've seen Emily catch her by the shoulders and shake her until her teeth rattled. Emily is a very strong person.'

'Didn't you say anything to her? I mean Emily?' Jean was surprised; it didn't sound like the way an old retainer would normally behave.

Elspeth hesitated. 'No. You see, Emily's always been with us, and in some ways she brought Moira up. So she's always had, well, an authority over her, and I wouldn't ever interfere in that.'

Jean wondered how much Douglas knew of this, and how hard he had questioned Emily.

'Had anything happened before Moira's death that might have particuarly upset Emily?'

'It could have been that whole Rory thing. Everybody knew how obsessed Rory was with Moira, and Emily really thought she was driving him mad.'

Elspeth raised her head as if she'd heard something. She got up, went quietly to the door, opened it suddenly and looked out. There was nobody in the corridor, and she looked suspiciously at the closed door opposite. 'I thought I heard a noise,' she said, coming back into her room and closing the door.

Jean wondered if spending so much time with Colin was having an effect on Elspeth's mind. She remembered patients with the *folie à deux* syndrome, a situation where two people living together went quietly, progressively and simultaneously mad.

'I sometimes think somebody's going to kill me,' said Elspeth.

'Why?'

'I really don't know. Sometimes . . . I feel somebody's stalking me.'

'Here? Inside the house?'

Elspeth thought about that. 'No, I don't think so,' she said. 'I walk quite a lot, sometimes in the woods, or down by the river. I hear twigs cracking behind me, and I call out to see who it is, but there's never any answer. Sometimes it's just a feeling, a tightness in my chest that tells me somebody is thinking about me and planning bad things.'

'Do you think someone was stalking Moira?'

'No. I think *that* happened suddenly, maybe even by accident . . .'

'Elspeth, you must have some reason for saying that,' said Jean earnestly. 'I don't see how it can be something you have guessed.'

Elspeth looked over Jean's head into the distance. 'You asked me what I *thought*,' she replied. 'And that's what I think.'

The window was open a few inches, and they heard the sound of a car's tyres scrunching in the gravel below. Elspeth went to the window. 'They're back,' she said, expressionlessly. Jean pulled aside the gauze curtain. Below was a grey Jaguar, looking sleek and out of place in the genteel, run-down forecourt. Behind the car, the dark trees guarded the river bank, now invisible in the fading light. Behind the trees, a light blinked and

Jean's hand went instinctively to her mouth. But she realized it was only somebody switching a light on in one of the cottages.

Chapter Twenty-one

Patricia was standing in the great hall, and Alastair walked in after her with Emily, both carrying luggage from the car. Emily, wearing her usual rather sullen expression, carried the two heaviest cases as if they were full of feathers, and Jean took another look at her strong, muscled body. Anybody unwise enough to attack Emily in a dark alley would get the shock of their lives and finish up the loser, she thought.

Patricia looked mildly surprised to see Jean, as she and Elspeth came down the stairs, although she had surely seen Jean's little Renault parked outside.

'Have you eaten?' Elspeth asked them. She was visibly nervous again, and her eyes went from Patricia to Alastair and back again.

'Dinner will be ready in one hour,' said Emily in a deep voice that indicated there would be trouble if they had already eaten.

Alastair pulled off his driving gloves and handed them to Emily without looking at her. He was watching Jean, not staring, of course, he was far too well-bred to do that, but nevertheless his gaze was questioning and unyielding.

'Jean came by to see Colin,' said Elspeth.

Alastair's lips tightened. 'I trust you found him no worse, doctor,' he said. 'I'm sure Lady Elspeth told you

that at present he is being treated by an Edinburgh
specialist.'

'I hope Dr Patel can do something for Sir Colin,' said
Jean, worried. 'I suppose he sees a lot of cases of that
kind.'

'I suppose he does,' said Alastair. He remained
polite, but was obviously waiting for Jean to leave.
Jean, who had a number of questions to ask him and
Patricia, decided that this might not be the best
moment, and left.

Her Renault looked shabby, small and friendly beside
the glistening Jaguar, and Jean got into it with a feeling
of relief mixed with anxiety. Her visit had raised at least
as many questions as had been answered, and a cloud of
sadness descended on her as she drove back into Perth.
The death of Moira Dalgleish was taking on certain
unexpected and rather frightening aspects.

'I don't want to bring you unnecessary publicity, Mr
Thierry,' Douglas was saying in his smoothest tones.
'But I do have a number of questions I'd like to ask you.
So I'd as soon meet you in some place other than your
home or your place of work.'

Armand, at his salon, was sweating and gripped the
phone hard. He had to handle this with great delicacy
and care, or his whole life would fatally unravel just
when things seemed to be settling down.

'Most kind and considerate of you, I am sure,' said
Armand, his French accent stronger than usual. 'Where
do you suggest, sir?'

'How about the Isle of Skye lounge?' said Doug, as if
it had just come into his mind. 'Tonight after dinner,
about nine?'

'I'll be there,' promised Armand, and after he put the
phone down, he sat and did some very hard thinking.

The Isle of Skye lounge was one of Douglas's
favourite places and he went there often enough to
know the people who worked behind the bar. Douglas

arrived at eight-thirty, and was glad to see that Long-Arm Samson was on duty. Nobody knew what his real name was, and his nickname came from his great strength which he occasionally demonstrated to the patrons. His best trick, lifting three men simultaneously off the floor, he usually reserved for rowdy customers. It not only impressed them with his strength, but he knew how to squeeze exactly the right amount of air out of their lungs to restore their sense of decorum.

Doug had a brief chat with Samson, then sat down with a small Macallan in his favourite booth, from which he could see the old bridge, the river, and the city lights going on as the sun went down over the trees lining the North Inch.

Armand came in fifteen minutes early, and Doug correctly ascribed that to nervousness. Douglas was expecting him to appear in some flamboyant outfit befitting a French beautician, and was surprised to see him in a conservative dark suit with a white shirt and a narrow, dark-blue tie. Armand looked around for a few moments, then came over to Douglas's booth and introduced himself.

'Get yourself a drink,' said Douglas, who had a reason for not getting it himself.

As Armand went towards the bar Doug nodded to Samson, who was polishing glasses behind the bar.

Armand came back with a lager and lime, considered something of a sissy drink in Douglas's circles.

Doug didn't give him time to have a single peaceful swallow. 'How well did you know Moira Dalgleish?' he asked in a voice that was louder than necessary.

'Slightly,' answered Armand. He looked around. 'Do you need to speak so loud? You said—'

' "Slightly"?' said Douglas in the same tone. 'Is having her to visit you at home in the middle of the night a *slight* acquaintance nowadays?'

'In the middle of the night?' Armand's look of astonishment was convincing. 'Sir, you are mistaken.

Miss Moira was a consultant, and we discussed her buying a share of my business. She made a number of visits to my house to discuss the matter. Of course, these visits were in the evenings, because I work during the day and I didn't want to meet her in the office.'

'Why not?' snapped Doug.

'For the same reasons we are meeting here, sir,' said Armand in a conciliatory tone. 'As you said, to avoid unnecessary publicity.'

'Mr Thierry,' said Douglas, prodding, 'we have reason to believe that you were engaged in a sexual liaison with Moira Dalgleish, and we suspect that there may be some link between that relationship and her death.'

To Doug's surprise, Armand seemed relieved, and sat back in the booth. He bobbed his glass to Douglas, said '*santé*', which Douglas assumed to be the French equivalent of 'cheers', and swallowed a dainty sip of lager. He put the glass down and dabbed his lips with a paper napkin.

'Inspector Niven,' said Armand, 'I have a confession to make.'

Doug's mouth opened slightly. He'd hardly even started to work on the man. 'I'm listening,' he said, repressing a professional urge to read Armand his rights.

'I have no interest in women,' said Armand. 'I find my personal fulfilment elsewhere.' Armand looked boldly at Douglas, who recoiled, although he realized that he shouldn't have been surprised. After all, the man was a beautician or whatever they called them, and a foreign one to boot. Like interior decorators and ballet dancers, he thought disgustedly, they're all poofters. Then Douglas realized he might be able to use the situation to his advantage.

He took a manly swig of Macallan and allowed his face to take on an expression of overt contempt. 'Do you know what a *poofter* is, Mr Thierry?' he said in a voice loud enough to cause the people in the next booth to turn around. 'I'll tell you what a poofter is, in case you don't know the other English words for it. A poofter is a filthy faggot, a bum-boy, a pervert, a catamite, a dirty buggerer . . .'

Armand stood up, red in the face, and for a second Douglas thought he was going to throw the drink in his face. Doug braced himself, but Armand merely slammed his glass down hard enough to splash beer on the table. He said something in French that Doug assumed was uncomplimentary, and left the lounge without another word.

As soon as Armand was safely gone, Douglas took out a large handkerchief, picked up Armand's glass by the base and examined it carefully. No question, even with the naked eye he could see good prints all over Samson's well-polished glass, including a full palm, made, Douglas concluded, at the height of Armand's anger. He stood up, went over to the bar, poured the remaining beer into the grating below the beer-pull, grinned at Samson, gave him a five-pound note and left. It didn't occur to him then that had Armand, in fact, been homosexual, he probably would not have been so outraged by the synonyms Douglas had used. In the car, Doug switched on the overhead light, placed the glass in a plastic evidence envelope, sealed it, and wrote the usual information on the label.

Doug realized that he might have been wasting his time with Armand Thierry, but by the time he turned the corner into the police garage, Doug's overall impression of the beautician was that he was a dangerous and disconcerting man.

Chapter Twenty-two

The doorbell rang and, for once, it was after the Montroses had finished dinner. The girls were watching television, Steven was dozing in his chair, and Jean was trying to catch up with her NHS paperwork, which was threatening to take up so much of her time and effort that there wouldn't be any left for her patients. Fiona went to the door, as always knowing Doug's ring, but this time she treated him just like one of the many ordinary visitors who came from time to time to the Montroses' house.

'It took the arrival of Douglas Junior for Fiona to get over him,' Lisbie whispered to her mother while Fiona was out of the room. 'It's really weird. Now Cathie's her best friend.'

Fiona led Douglas into the living room, so that the conversation wouldn't wake her father, and with a sigh Jean put away her papers, got up and turned down the volume on the television. When Lisbie started to complain, Jean pointed soundlessly at Steven.

Douglas was looking listless, and rubbed the top of his head with the palm of his hand; a sure sign that all was not well.

'How's Cathie doing?' asked Jean, feeling guilty because she hadn't been to see her that day. Cathie had

made very good progress and had been allowed home
the day before.

'Fine,' replied Doug. 'She got up today a couple of
times, but she's weak yet. And the baby's no' quite
ready to come home, and she misses him.'

'Fiona's been spending a lot of time with her,' said
Jean. 'We're lucky if she comes home for meals.'

'Cathie's very grateful,' said Doug. He paused for a
moment and grinned a bit sheepishly. 'It's amazing how
she's changed. I mean Fiona.'

'Tell Cathie I'll stop by tomorrow,' said Jean, who
didn't want to talk now about Fiona's reactions to
Cathie's baby, psychologically interesting though the
topic might be. Also she knew that Doug hadn't come to
talk to her about Cathie or Fiona.

'How's the Moira Dalgleish case coming along?' Jean
reached into her basket and pulled out her knitting. The
needles were spiked into the ball of baby blue wool like
two daggers.

'We're not exactly ready to make an arrest,' replied
Doug wryly. 'In fact, the more people I see in
connection with this case, the more confused I get.'

'Who, for instance?' asked Jean, busy setting up her
knitting; a little jacket for Douglas Niven Junior.

Douglas usually found that talking about his cases
with Jean helped him sort out his own thoughts, almost
as if he were holding them up to some kind of mirror.

'All of them,' he said. 'And on top of everything we
have the Scottish Office interfering. They've been
breathing down our necks on this case right from the
beginning. They want us to make a quick arrest, but
they don't want us bothering the Dalgleishes. And the
family's given us no help whatsoever. You'd think that
with their only daughter being killed they'd at least try,
wouldn't you?'

Jean didn't say anything for a few moments as her
knitting was approaching a critical juncture. She'd had
to take down the turn at the shoulder once already, and

didn't want to have to do it a second time.

'I suppose as Alastair's an MP they want to protect him,' she said. 'One of the perks of public service, I suppose. In any case, I don't imagine the Dalgleishes could be much help, do you?'

There was something in Jean's tone that made Doug stare at her for a second, but his head was so full of anxiety about the lack of progress in the case that he just went on.

'OK,' he said. 'This is the way I've been thinking.' He held up three fingers. 'We have three headings,' he said, 'motive, opportunity, ability. Starting with the motive, I think we can rule out money.' He glanced at Jean. 'Well, can't we?' he asked, his voice defensive. 'Moira Dalgleish wasn't rich, and as far as I know she didn't have any inheritance somebody might have had their eye on.'

'I'm not sure that you can ever rule out money,' said Jean quietly, 'but go on.'

'Well, Jean,' said Douglas, feeling increasingly hemmed in, 'I'm no' about to go through the entire list of possible murder motives that exist in the human mind.' His Glaswegian accent was strengthening, as it was prone to do when he came under pressure.

'How about looking at it the other way round,' suggested Jean sensibly. 'Rather than trying to fit people into the motives, it might be easier to look at the individuals and see what motives they might have had.' She felt very glad that she wasn't under the kind of pressures that were being exerted on Douglas.

'I suppose our number one suspect has to be Rory McDermott, then,' said Doug. 'He got out of hospital a few days ago. You know he tried to kill his bidie-in, don't you?'

'I heard something about it,' said Jean. 'Bella came down to the surgery for me to look at her neck, but she wouldn't say anything about what happened. She certainly sticks by her man.'

'Jealousy, I would think,' said Doug, biting on a piece of cuticle. 'And rage. That could have been his motive.'

Jean moved in her chair. 'How do you think it happened? Do you think he went up to Dalgleish House, somehow managed to get inside, strangled Moira, dragged her out and threw her into the river?'

'No. I dinna think that.' Doug sat back. He had obviously considered the possible sequence of events very carefully. 'He must have phoned her and asked her to meet him down by the river. According to Kevin Marshall, that's where they used to meet when they were having their affair, about a quarter of a mile up from the cottages. You know she had a reputation for being daring, even foolhardy on occasion. And maybe she couldn't resist having him beg her to return, or maybe he had something she wanted from him.'

'What about that lure you found on her body?' asked Jean.

'Symbolism,' said Doug. He wasn't really comfortable with the word, and it showed. 'He stuck the hook in her as a symbolic gesture.'

'You don't think his story is true, then? About going fishing and accidently hooking on to her body?'

'It's not that I dinna believe him,' said Douglas, 'It's simply that I dinna like coincidences. Still . . . If what he says really happened, her body would have come down with the current and stuck in the roots by the pool where we found her. Then he happens to go fishing a week later . . .' Douglas came as close to a grin as he'd come that evening. 'If that's the way it happened,' he said, 'that must have given him about as nasty a shock as anybody could ever get.'

'In that case he wouldn't have known for sure who it was he'd found,' said Jean. 'Although I suppose he might have guessed.'

'The story was in all the papers, the day she disappeared.'

'Do you think he would have told Bella?'

Douglas shrugged. 'Still assuming his story was true, I suppose he'd have been so shaken up when he got home that yes, he would have told her.'

'And then she went out to the phone box to call the police,' said Jean in a musing tone. 'I don't know, Douglas. That's not what I'd do if Steven knocked off some ex-ladyfriend of his.'

Doug's mouth opened slightly and he stared at Jean. 'Steven?' he said wonderingly. 'If he . . .well, if he did, then what *would* you do?'

'I'd probably be rather pleased,' said Jean, after considering the possibility for a moment. 'And I certainly wouldn't run out to call you.'

Jean returned to her knitting, an amused expression on her face.

'You know, Jean,' said Doug, coming back to the main topic of discussion, 'it always struck me that Moira was an unlikely candidate for a murder victim. A young mother with a baby to look after — living at home, not leading a riotous life or bothering anyone.'

'She was hardly your typical everyday Mum, though, was she?' asked Jean mildly. 'She had quite a reputation, even after she got married and had the baby. When she came back, it seemed to start all over again, as if she couldn't do without a man. Men, I mean.'

'Apparently she was quite a *seductress*,' said Douglas, putting strong emphasis on the last word. 'Every man was a challenge, and as soon as she got one where she wanted him, she'd move on to the next.'

'That's what Elspeth said.'

There was silence for a few moments; Jean had found a hole in her knitting and had to unravel a few rows. Douglas watched the process with interest.

'So, who followed in Rory McDermott's, er, footsteps?' asked Jean once the defect had been repaired.

Douglas told Jean about Sandra Cowie and how she

had told Jamieson about her neighbour Armand
Thierry's nocturnal adventures with Moira.

'Armand? Really?' Jean was astonished. 'He's my
hairdresser.'

'That is hardly a guarantee of innocence,' said
Douglas as if he had read the phrase somewhere. He
crossed his legs, then recrossed them. 'Jean, do you
think he's . . . gay?' he asked, slightly embarrassed to
be asking a woman such a question.

'Do you mean homosexual?' asked Jean. 'To me, gay
still means cheerful, glad, exuberant, that kind of thing.
Armand, homosexual?' Jean considered the matter for
a moment. 'Hard to tell, Douglas. With some men it's
easy: the way of walking, the hand movements and the
sing-song voice, but often I just can't tell. With women,
I usually can't tell until I've spoken to them for a while,
and to tell you the truth it doesn't usually cross my
mind. As for Armand . . . I don't think so, but I could
easily be wrong. Why?'

'He told me he was,' replied Doug. 'But I think it was
just to put us off the track.'

'You think he might have killed Moira?'

'I'm really grabbing at straws,' said Doug, beginning
to sound desperate. 'There's so little to go on. He says
he had a purely business relationship with her, but his
neighbour, Sandra, says Moira used to visit him at
night, and at the time of her death she wasn't seeing any
other man that we know of or that the family knows of.
So she and Armand could have had some kind of lovers'
quarrel, I suppose. She could have been giving him the
heave-ho, as she did with Rory. And you know what
those hot-blooded Frenchmen are like.'

Jean considered the matter. 'I'm sure Armand isn't
homosexual,' she said. 'I was thinking about the way he
acts with the female members of his staff. I'd guarantee
he's as heterosexual as they come.'

'That was my impression,' said Douglas, relieved.

'By the way, Douglas, you know that accent he has?'

Jean paused while she switched to the other sleeve of the little jacket. 'Some days it's more pronounced than others, and it doesn't always ring true — I've occasionally wondered if it could be fake.'

'We're in the process of checking him out. We should soon know for sure.'

The door opened and Fiona looked in. 'Would anybody like some tea?' she asked. 'I just made some and I was going to bring it through.'

'Good idea,' said Jean. 'You'll find shortbread and some Penguins in the tin.'

A couple of minutes later, Lisbie appeared, and Fiona followed her with the tea things. Steven was still asleep and they hadn't wanted to wake him.

'I know I shouldn't,' said Jean, unwrapping the red-and-gold foil of a second chocolate biscuit. 'I just can't resist them.'

Doug, who had a fetish about keeping himself in shape, flexed his muscles and said, 'Jean, have you ever thought of running?'

'Don't be silly, Douglas.' Jean poured the tea while her mind had gone on to thinking about Alastair Dalgleish and his political aspirations. 'You know I'm not interested in politics.'

Doug stared at her for a moment, a piece of shortbread half-way to his mouth. 'I meant *running* running,' he said after a moment. 'You know, for exercise.'

'Good heavens, of course not,' said Jean, indignantly. 'Can you imagine me galloping around in a skin-tight Lycra suit? They'd lock me up for disturbing the peace.'

'It was just a thought,' muttered Douglas, going bright pink at the awe-inspiring image Jean had just conjured up for him. Fiona and Lisbie howled with laughter at the idea.

A few moments later Steven appeared at the door, his mouth already open to complain about the noise they

were making. When he saw Doug, he mumbled
something about going up to bed, and disappeared.

The girls took the tea things away soon after, and
Douglas became morose again. Jean picked up her
knitting. The jacket was almost finished, except for the
decorative blue ribbon that would go around the waist
and cuffs.

'Have you ruled out all the Dalgleishes?' she asked.
'And the other people in the household?'

'I haven't ruled out anybody,' replied Doug, who was
beginning to feel frustrated and irritable. 'As for the
household, is there anybody else besides Emily?'

'I'm sorry,' said Jean. 'I was thinking of that chap,
Kevin something.'

'Marshall,' said Doug. 'He and Maggie were away at
her sister's in Arbroath, so that's not even a possibility.'

Jean nodded absent-mindedly. A number of things
were coming together in her head concerning the
Dalgleishes and she wished Douglas would go home and
let her think her thoughts through.

'Did you ever talk to Emily?' she asked.

'Just to ask her if she'd seen or heard anything
suspicious the night Moira disappeared,' replied Doug,
surprised. 'Why?'

'I believe she's on good terms with Kevin. And, of
course, she's related to Rory McDermott. Cousins, or
something like that. She's certainly got the same muscle
power. Did you notice how strong she is?' Jean was
threading the silky blue ribbon in and out of the jacket,
and wondering if it was going to be wide enough. 'I
don't imagine Emily was involved, I just wondered if
you'd thought about her.'

'Not particularly,' said Doug, who obviously thought
there were other more likely suspects. 'But thanks for
adding another name.' He grinned sadly. 'Jean, I'm
really stuck. I don't have a decent motive, there's half a
dozen people who could have done it, but nobody in
particular stands out. And the brass is breathing down

my neck, demanding results. Bob McLeod's smoking his pipe as if he's heading for a meltdown, and the Chief Superintendent calls me every day, mostly because somebody's been after him on the phone. I'm going to have to make an arrest soon, and I'm beginning to think that Rory McDermott's going to be the one.'

'I have to agree,' said Jean, but she didn't sound totally convinced. 'Right now he does look like the most likely suspect. There's a motive of sorts, he's a violent individual, and, of course, you found his lure on her body.' She hesitated. 'Douglas, do you think you could hold off pulling him in for a couple of days? I should be hearing something tomorrow that might shed some light.'

'What are you up to, Jean?' he asked, suspicion blending uncomfortably with relief. But Jean wouldn't say anything more, and Douglas got up and went on his way soon after.

Fiona said goodnight to him at the door but didn't escort him to his car the way she usually did, and in a strange way he missed it.

Chapter Twenty-three

When Alastair, Patricia and Elspeth Dalgleish finished dinner, Emily cleared the table and went upstairs, grumbling to herself, to collect Sir Colin's tray and take it back down to the kitchen. After doing the dishes, she put on her outdoor shoes and coat and went through the kitchen garden back to her cottage. Since Moira's death, Alastair had suggested that she take a torch and a whistle with her when going to and from her cottage, but she had just snorted.

'If anybody I don't know comes anywhere near me,' she said, her eyes glittering, 'I'll kill 'em.'

The cottage was dark and humid, but Emily didn't notice. She'd lived there for many years and the damp never bothered her. There was a little wall-clock above the sink, and she switched on the kitchen-light just long enough to read the time and pick up her shopping bag, which contained a batch of scones she'd made early that morning.

The bus to town would be stopping in front of the main gates in five minutes.

Emily locked the front door of the cottage and headed up the service drive, where black ruts had formed on either side of the snow-covered surface. The light cast long, slate-blue shadows across the snow and, beyond the river, an orange-yellow glow from the

setting sun backlit the tracery of bare, black trees
clustered along the river bank. A chilling wind blew
around her lisle stockings, but she didn't notice; she was
thinking about the night Moira had disappeared.

She changed buses in Perth, and it was quite dark by
the time Emily arrived at Rory's house and rang the
bell. She was astonished when Bella opened the door.

'I thought you'd be long gone by now, bitch,' said
Emily, pushing past her into the small living room. Rory
was sitting on the couch, with two pillows behind him,
watching television. He didn't look up. 'Leave her
alone, Emily,' he said. 'She did what was best for
everybody.'

'Like stabbing you?'

'Ach, well,' said Rory, a man of few words. 'You'd
likely have done the same, under the circumstances.
Anyway I wasna' talking about that.'

'I keep telling you, I didn't kill her,' said Bella,
pulling on a strand of hair, but her voice was drowned
out by Rory.

'Shut the hell up, woman,' he said. 'Me and Emily
both know, so don't bother telling us any different.
Emily saw you up there the night Moira was killed.'

'I told you, I just went up to the house to talk to
her—'

'Some talk,' said Emily, glaring at Bella.

'Well, I know my way around because I worked
there,' continued Bella doggedly, 'and I didn't think
there was anybody around, then I ran into Mr Alastair
in the big hall.'

'Yeah, sure,' said Rory, grinning, 'I bet. So what did
he say?'

'Well, he says to me, "What are you doing here,
Bella", and I says to him, "I'm come to see Emily",
and he laughs, seeing my face because he could tell I
hadn't come to see Emily, and he says, "She's
downstairs in the kitchens, not up here", so I went

down and of course you weren't there so I left through the back.'

'Moira must have been right heavy,' said Emily, eyeing Bella. 'How did you manage?'

In answer, Bella slammed the door and vanished into the kitchen, while Rory and Emily turned back to the television programme and watched it for a few minutes without saying anything. It was a comedy, and each time Rory laughed, he followed it up with a painful cough from the healing incision in his chest.

'Why don't you change the channel?' asked Emily. 'Turn to BBC, that'll stop you laughing.'

'That Bella,' said Rory reflectively, 'she's all right really, considering she's just a woman.'

'You made it up with her?'

He didn't answer for a while; on the screen a fisherman had caught an imaginary big fish that not only refused to die but started to argue with him.

'Yep. We're doing fine. What she did to Moira . . . Well, I suppose it was all for the best, in the long run.'

Silence followed that remark for several minutes.

'Why doesn't she want to admit it? To you, anyway?'

Rory shrugged. 'Maybe she still thinks I might kill her if I knew for sure she'd done it.'

The comedy sketch was ending; the fish was throwing the fisherman back into the water.

'They're probably going to arrest me,' said Rory when the programme was over and he'd switched the set off. He coughed again. 'If they do, I'm going to confess.'

Emily jumped up from her chair and caught Rory by the shoulder. 'You're going to *what*?' she screamed. Then she understood, and broke into a deep-throated guffaw.

'It's amazing,' said Doug, scratching the top of his head. 'I've never known anybody with so little recorded

information about them.' And, in fact, the information
on Armand Thierry was less than slender. The
computer, which could normally be expected to come
up with a substantial folio on suspects, had come up
with little more than his age and address.

'Maybe he's one of these informers,' suggested
Jamieson. 'You know, the ones who have to get a new
identity from the government.'

'Jamieson, this is Scotland, no' the United States,'
said Doug wearily. 'Did the fingerprint people come up
with anything?'

'No, sir.'

The atmosphere subsided once again to its morose
level.

The phone rang.

'Answer it,' said Doug without looking up.

After a few moments, Jamieson put his hand over the
mouthpiece. 'It's the central fingerprint lab,' he said,
his voice full of excitement. 'They've just got a report in
from Interpol . . .' He rolled the name off his tongue as
if he'd just been invited to head the agency. Doug
snatched the phone from him, but it was only a
secretary who said she would be faxing a report to them.
A mistake had been made by the Tayside Police, she
said accusingly. The prints they had sent were of a man
named Roger Van Polt, wanted for murder in South
Africa. They had no records of any kind on anyone with
the name of Armand Thierry.

For the next couple of hours, Douglas's office was a
flurry of activity. Douglas informed the Chief
Superintendent of this new development, and Bob
McLeod came down to help. Bob had a reputation for
knowing at least one person on every English-speaking
police force in the world and, sure enough, he had an
acquaintance in the Cape Town police department.

Although it was two hours ahead there, and most of
them had gone home, their South African colleagues
were very cooperative. They tracked down a couple of

records-department people, and within an hour a fax
came through to Perth with all the details of Roger Van
Polt and the murder he had been accused of. Bob was
still on the phone to Cape Town, so Doug got to the fax
first. He read that Van Polt's wife had not drowned, as
had been reported to the authorities, but, according to
the autopsy report, she had been strangled and was
already dead by the time she hit the water.

There was a major problem, however. The
photograph of Van Polt that accompanied the file
didn't look anything like Thierry.

On the phone, Bob's Cape Town friend, Chief
Inspector Simon Boerhaave, was extremely excited. 'We
haven't been on the best of terms with our local press,'
he said, 'and they gave us a real hard time over the Van
Polt business. So we need to get him back as badly as I
need beer on a Friday night.'

Doug came in with the next fax sheet, and Bob gave
him a preoccupied nod.

'I'll come and get him,' Boerhaave was saying. 'Just
as soon as you get the extradition papers filed. I'll come
a couple of days early, bring my clubs and we can play
Gleneagles, right?'

'There's been some kind of mix-up,' whispered Doug,
holding up the faxed photograph for Bob to see. 'This is
a different man.'

'Fingerprints never lie,' said Bob, his hand over the
mouthpiece, but he was obviously shaken. 'Actually, we
may want Van Polt here,' he told Boerhaave cautiously.
'He happens to be a suspect in a murder case in Perth.
We don't have that much on him at the present time, so
don't buy your air ticket just yet.'

Boerhaave promised to send faxes of all remaining
material they had on Van Polt and, in return, Bob
assured him that he'd keep them informed of their
progress.

His telephone pre-empted by Bob McLeod, Douglas
rather grumblingly went to the next-door office to make

his own calls. At the back of his mind was the question
of how Armand Thierry/Roger Van Polt had managed
to circumvent the immigration mechanisms which
existed to prevent exactly this kind of thing from
happening.

Jock Nairn, he thought, Jock the comic. Jock had
worked in immigration so long that he knew all the
tricks people employed to get into the country via the
back door. Doug reached him after several attempts.
One of the things that long service had taught Jock was
where to hide when he didn't feel like talking to anyone,
but his voice perked up when he heard Douglas.

'Well,' he said, 'The Very Reverend Douglas Niven!
Talk about a voice from the past! Now I'm sure you just
called to say hello and find out how Diane and the kids
are doing, right? Well, Diane had a hysterectomy last
year, but it took a while for her to get back on her feet,
and both girls graduated from Cambridge last year . . .'

'I'm delighted to hear it, Jock,' interrupted Doug,
grinning to himself. 'Do give my regards to Diane and
the girls.'

'Diane?' shouted Jock in mock anger. 'Who's Diane?
What girls? You know I'm a life-long bachelor and
don't appreciate that kind if talk, especially from a man
of the cloth such as yourself. Now what can I do for
you?'

Doug explained about Armand Thierry, also known
as Roger Van Polt.

'When do you think he entered this country?' asked
Jock; all business now.

'The first stuff on his sheet was about four years ago,'
replied Doug. 'So it could have been around then,
maybe March or April.'

There was a brief silence. 'Wait until I go to another
phone,' said Jock in a different voice, and a few seconds
later there was a click as the first phone was hung up.

'Did you not hear about the wee scandal we had here,
Douglas?' asked Jock in a quiet voice. 'There was a fine

rio of people here who were selling passports, legal ones, of course, entry visas, all kinds of things that certain people are happy to pay a very high price for. Anyway, this was discovered only about three years ago, but it had been going on quietly for almost five years before that.'

'How did it work?' asked Douglas.

'I'm not going to tell you all the details in case you get any ideas,' replied Jock, 'but basically they operated the scam on a three-tier level. The passport applications went through the normal channels to a chap on the first level, using names that the applicants had been instructed to use. In the correct course of events, these particular applications would have been rejected there and then, but they were processed in the usual way. Then they went to the second tier, where these things get approved or rejected. They were approved, of course, and passed upwards to the final implementation stage where our third lad was waiting with his pile of passports and a rubber stamp.'

'That's organization for you,' said Douglas admiringly. 'Are those lads in jail now?'

Jock gave a brief, disgusted laugh. 'Are you joking? The cover-up was as efficient as their scheme. They paid off all the right people, nobody could prove anything, and the only thing that happened was that they all left the department, as wealthy men, need I add. And all three went to better-paid and more important jobs, as one might expect.'

'It's a good lesson for you,' said Douglas. 'Maybe if you play your cards right you won't need to work until you drop dead or retire.'

'If I'd been caught doing that at my level,' said Jock grimly, 'my testicles would right now be hanging on the wall in the Minister's office.'

'Well, Jock,' said Douglas in a rare flight of barrack-room humour, 'the size they are, nobody would ever notice.'

'Anyway, your lad could have got into the country that way,' said Jock, ignoring Doug's last remark. 'It would have cost him upwards of ten thousand pounds, but plenty of people can afford that, I suppose.'

Is there any way we can prove it? Serial numbers, that kind of thing?'

'On passports, there's a six-digit number preceded and followed by single letters. In most of the suspect ones, the last letter is D.'

'Thanks, Jock. We can check that easily enough. And, by the way, give Diane a big fat kiss from me!'

Chapter Twenty-four

The surgery was so busy that Jean didn't have time even to think about Moira Dalgleish until after the last patient had gone. Eleanor came in with a batch of forms to be signed.

'Could you bring me in a cup of tea?' asked Jean. 'With a piece of that fruitcake that Mrs Armstrong brought in last week.'

'It's all gone,' replied Eleanor, and Jean felt a surge of annoyance, partly because she felt hungry and because, as Helen never ate fruitcake, Eleanor must have eaten it or taken it home.

She shrugged. 'All right, some digestives, then, please.'

'They're all gone too,' said Eleanor. 'There's nothing except some old Rich Tea biscuits.'

Helen came in, ready to go for her weekly constitutional around the North Inch. Once, she'd invited Jean to go with her, and Jean had to trot to keep up with her Olympian pace and took two days to recover.

'We're getting a visit from the high heid yins in Dundee next Tuesday,' announced Helen in a calm voice.

It always surprised Jean that Helen, normally a forthright, opinionated and occasionally intolerant woman, should be so astonishingly passive when it came to the bureaucrats of the NHS. 'For the size of our practice,' Helen went on, 'our waiting room is almost three square-metres too small, according to their calculations. So a delegation is coming to determine if the surgery should be closed down in the interests of the public health.'

'That's a load of rubbish.' Jean was furious. 'Typical waste of public time and money. Our waiting room's been the same size for ever. And nobody's ever complained, that I know of, and in any case there's no way we can make it any bigger.'

'Well, Jean,' said Helen in a curious voice, 'all of this is going to be on your shoulders soon.'

Surprised, Jean looked at her long-time partner, who in turn glared at Eleanor. 'What are you looking at?' she demanded. Eleanor stammered something inaudible and hurried out of the room.

'I'm going to retire,' said Helen. 'In three months. I'm having a lot of trouble with my back, and I'm so tired of fighting with the stupid NHS bureaucracy that I've finally had enough.'

Jean was speechless. Helen, her old friend and partner . . . She couldn't believe it. She got up, and hugged Helen for a long time. It was an emotional moment, and both women wept a little.

After Helen went off towards the North Inch, Jean sat down and thought about the changes that Helen's departure would entail. Life would be very different without her; Helen was a mine of medical information and often helped with factual matters, whereas Jean's strength was in her ability to relate to her patients and understand the causes behind their complaints and ailments. And then there was the whole business of dealing with the NHS people. Ever since she joined Helen's practice all those years ago, Jean had happily left the form-filling, the responding to meaningless and obscure questionnaires, and worst of all, dealing with

the uninformed former nurses-turned-minor-admini-
strators now in positions of power in the system. All
that she had left to Helen, and the thought that she
would now have to spend all that time coping with the
bureaucracy instead of helping her patients filled her
with panic.

Eleanor knocked on the door and waited to be told to
come in; something that Jean did not remember Eleanor
ever doing before. Somehow she had found a piece of
fruitcake and some digestive biscuits, which she now
presented with Jean's tea on a small wooden tray. There
was even a little doily on the plate.

'My goodness,' said Jean, observing this sudden
departure from Eleanor's usual off-hand behaviour.
'News travels fast around here, doesn't it?'

'Yes, doctor.'

Jean hardly recognized the respectful tone of her
secretary's voice. 'Eleanor,' she said, capitalizing on
this new and unexpected behaviour, 'I have a number of
phone calls to make and I don't want to be disturbed, all
right?'

'Yes, doctor,' replied Eleanor obediently, and Jean
started to wonder if she preferred her previous attitude
to this subservient one. 'Would you care for some more
tea? And I found a couple of Penguins in the tin.'

Jean hesitated only for a fraction of a second before
saying no. When Eleanor left the room, Jean opened
her desk drawer, took out a small list of telephone
numbers and put them on the desk.

The first call was to the London photographic studio
she had phoned the day before.

The friendly young man she had spoken to was just as
helpful, but this time he was a little puzzled. 'We don't
have any record of Donald Glashan being photographed
here, Dr Montrose. I'm pretty sure, because I went back
over our records for the last three years.'

'I hate to think I gave you all that work,' said Jean,
feeling very remorseful and guilty.

'It took three minutes,' said the young man
cheerfully. 'All our records are on the computer now.'

'Oh, good.' Jean paused for a second and took a deep
breath. 'Then whose portrait was that, the one whose
number I sent you?'

'Oh, that,' said the young man. 'That was a publicity
photograph for a young man by the name of Johnny
King, an actor. We took it six years ago, and made fifty
copies. It's the only portrait we ever did of him, so I
don't suppose he was very successful.'

Jean thanked him and put the phone down very
slowly. It was all beginning to come together now and
she felt a pervasive sadness seeping through her entire
body.

Douglas flipped over the enlarged photograph of Roger
Van Polt and looked on the back. The Cape Town
police had sent it via a special fax process to the central
computing station in Glasgow and it had been hand-
delivered from there. It had a rubber-stamped date, the
logo of the Cape Town CID, his handwritten full name,
Roger Spurling Van Polt and, below that, his date of
birth.

Doug passed the photograph to Bob McLeod. It
didn't bare even the slightest resemblance to Armand
Thierry, whose nose was fatter, lips wider, and
cheekbones higher. Even the chin was different;
whereas Armand had a dainty, almost feminine chin,
Roger Van Polt's heavy jaw dominated his face.

'Not a chance,' Doug sighed.

'Did you ever see before-and-after pictures of
Michael Jackson?' asked Bob, leaning back and
tamping his pipe. 'Before his plastic surgery, he looked
just like any other little black boy. Afterwards, he
looked like any other little white girl!'

'Amazing,' said Doug, still not convinced that such a
radical change could ever be made in a person's

appearance. Bob started his countdown routine before firing up his pipe and it made Doug yearn for a cigarette.

'Do we have enough to pull him in?'

'For the South Africans, yes. For us . . .' Doug would have dearly have liked to say yes, but in fact they had nothing. 'All we have is his fingerprints. There weren't any of his prints in her room, her car or on any of her belongings.'

'Nobody saw him hanging around Dalgleish House? Didn't the girls in his salon ever see him and Moira argue?'

Discouraged, Doug shook his head.

'Nothing,' he said.

'Did you check her address book?' A mushroom cloud of Balkan Sobranie smoke rose and flattened against the ceiling. 'Maybe Thierry was listed under "studs".'

'I don't think so.' Doug reached into his desk where he kept Moira's address book in its plastic evidence envelope, pulled it out and started to flip through the pages once again.

'Nope. There's nothing here we can tie him to. Not a name, a phone number, anything.' Douglas came to the last page, the long row of dates and figures headed by the letters RSVP. He'd gone over it several times, but couldn't make out what it referred to. 'This is the only thing I can't work out, Bob,' he said, passing him the little book, his thumb keeping it open at the last page. 'It must be a list of people she had to write back to, or something like that. I checked with the telephone numbers, but none of them correspond.'

Bob held the book at arm's length. 'I'm going to need glasses soon,' he said grumpily. 'It looks like a list of money,' he said. 'My wife does the same thing with her Bingo winnings.'

'Why RSVP?'

'Maybe it's money she owes people,' said Bob. 'Good luck to them if they try to collect now.'

Doug's eyes fell once again on the photograph, and he felt as if something had just exploded inside his head.

He jumped up so suddenly that his chair tipped over and Bob, startled, dropped his pipe on the table.

'Look!' shouted Douglas, stabbing his finger at the back of the photograph. 'Roger Spurling Van Polk! RSVP! She knew who he was! She must have been blackmailing him!'

Chapter Twenty-five

When he could, Jamieson liked to go dancing on Saturday nights, and the place he liked to go to was the Electric Whispers in Canal Street. The music was good, and, as one might expect from its name, not too loud. The girl at the desk smiled at him when he bought his ticket; Jamieson was a regular, although few of the staff knew that he was a policeman. He was a big, fine-looking man, if a little slow-moving, and invariably attracted the attention of the young women who frequented the place.

He went over to the bar and sat sideways so that he could watch the action. The lights were dim except on the dance floor, and it took his eyes a few moments to accommodate.

Jamieson had barely sat down when the seat next to him was taken. 'Hello, Mr Jamieson.'

Jamieson peered at the young woman and recognized Sandra Cowie, Armand Thierry's neighbour.

'Oh, hello,' he replied, then looked away. He'd thought about Sandra several times since his visit to her house, and had wondered rather pleasurably if he'd see her here. But now that she was sitting next to him, and evidently only too anxious to make his unprofessional acquaintance, Jamieson felt the usual discomfort he experienced when physically close to a woman, and the inner sinews of his body tightened up with apprehension.

'Would you like to buy me a drink?' asked Sandra in a seductive voice.

'All right,' said Jamieson, trying to hide his reluctance. The drinks here were not particularly cheap, and there wasn't much leeway in a constable's salary.

'Just a lemonade, please.' She eyed him hungrily in the gloom, sensing his discomfort and wondering what she could do or say to make him feel more relaxed.

They danced a couple of times, but the place was getting crowded and noisy. It was difficult to talk at the bar, where Jamieson carefully nursed a small Dewar's.

'Let's go back to my house,' said Sandra in his ear. 'I have most of a bottle of Dewar's, and we won't have to shout at each other.'

Jamieson hesitated for a moment, but let himself be persuaded. Fifteen minutes later, they were sitting very close together on Sandra's sofa, Jamieson holding a big tumbler full of scotch, whilst Sandra gently slid her hand up and down the inside of his thigh.

There was a muffled noise outside, like a car door being closed with care, and Sandra, surprised, got up and went to the window.

After a second she turned her head. 'Turn out the light!' she whispered urgently to Jamieson. Startled, he jumped up and did so, then joined her at the window.

They saw a man, barely visible in the gloom, creeping stealthily between them and the house next door, then they saw another following him.

'My God!' said Jamieson, his eyes wide. 'Burglars!' He turned to phone headquarters for reinforcements, when Sandra called to him again. 'Look!' she said, 'Isn't that Inspector Niven?'

Jamieson almost ran back to the window. Sandra caught his hand and held on to it tightly. Sure enough, to his utter astonishment, he saw Doug standing on the pavement opposite, facing the house. There was just enough light from the lamp-post for him to be clearly recognizable, and Jamieson saw that he was speaking into a portable radio.

Jamieson's first thought was that his boss was coming after him because he'd broken the rules and gone out with a woman who might at some point be a witness. Then he saw the shadowy figure of Bob McLeod join Doug, and he realized that he must be in the deepest trouble possible.

'Well,' he said, turning away from the window and bravely squaring his shoulders. 'I'm afraid this is the end of our evening, Sandra. I'd better go out before they come and break down your front door.'

At that moment, there was a crash and someone shouted; bright lights suddenly went on in the street, shining not at them but on the house next door, Armand Thierry's home.

'My God!' said Jamieson, appalled and angry. 'They're going after that hairdresser fellow! Without me!'

He rushed to the back door and charged outside, running with a speed and agility rare in a man of his size. He heard something crash through the hedge in front of him and, a moment later, ran smack into a person, with such a force he heard all the air coming out of him. They both crashed to the ground, Jamieson holding on tight, and shouting at the top of his voice.

Next morning, a photograph of Jamieson, clutching an obviously terrified man, was on the front page of the *Perth Courier*, above the caption: Police Hero Captures Foreign Killer.

Douglas was in his office with Bob McLeod, and Jamieson was standing with his back against the door because there wasn't room for him anywhere else.

'Just how the hell did you happen to be there?' asked

an exasperated Doug Niven, tapping the newspaper on his desk. 'We tried to reach you, but your mother said you were out *dancing*.'

Jamieson, knowing the trouble he's be in if he confessed to being with Sandra Cowie, said lamely that he just happened to be taking a walk in the neighbourhood, and by sheer chance landed up in the right place at the right time.

'Well, for the purposes of the report,' said Bob, looking at the ceiling, 'you were a member of the arrest team. It is not necessary to mention the fact that you were off duty at the time. Do you understand?'

'Yes, sir,' said Jamieson.

'That means keep your mouth shut and don't talk to the press or the TV or anybody else about last night's raid, all right?' said Douglas, who had learned from bitter experience that when dealing with Jamieson every 't' had to be crossed and every 'i' dotted.

The phone rang and Doug picked it up, while he continued to stare suspiciously at Jamieson, trying to figure out what really happened the night before.

'Jock, good morning.' That was the entire extent of Douglas's participation in the telephone conversation, but Bob saw his expression change first to astonishment and then to triumph.

'Well, I'll be damned,' he said when he put the phone down.

'Nobody'll disagree with that,' grunted Bob, but Doug's mind was far away, rearranging his thoughts.

'You aren't going to believe this,' he said finally. 'That was Jock Nairn at Immigration. He was calling from his home,' Doug paused; things were still clicking into place in his mind. 'OK . . .' Doug leaned back. 'I called him when we couldn't find out anything concerning Van Polk, and he told me that several years ago they'd found out that a little group of three senior people in his department had been selling immigration documents, but the whole thing was hushed up and the three officials left the department.' Douglas paused again, and looked from Jamieson to Bob, who was impatiently busying himself with his pipe.

'So?'

'Well, Jock has just told me who the three senior officials were.'

'For God's sake, Niven, get on with it,' said Bob, looking at his watch.

'Of those three,' said Douglas impressively, 'one is now the Scottish Secretary, the second a member of the Cabinet, and the third, the one who kept all the records, is our old friend Alastair Dalgleish.'

Bob, who was lighting his pipe, was so shocked that he accidentally inhaled a lungful of smoke and began to cough violently.

'My God,' he wheezed, finally, his eyes watering. 'That's the last link. That's how Moira happened to know about Van Polk. She must have gone through his papers . . .' Bob started to cough again, and his face turned purple.

'Fetch him a glass of water, Jamieson,' said Douglas.

Five minutes later, when Bob had fully recovered, the three of them clattered down the back stairs to the basement cells to see how Roger Van Polk was doing, before going on to the press conference which had been scheduled for 10 a.m., in time for the midday news reports.

The cells were crowded and the prisoners unusually noisy, because there was only one constable assigned to warder duty.

'He's in cell five,' said the harassed constable, in response to Bob's question. 'Could you get somebody to help me out here, sir? They're all needing water or something and I can't do it all myself.'

'Why don't you just sit down and have a good cry,' said the unsympathetic Superintendent. 'That is, after you've let us into cell five.'

They marched along the cell-lined corridor in single

file, in order of rank, to the accompaniment of yells and catcalls from the inmates, until they came to the end cell. Roger Van Polk was asleep on his bed, with his back turned to the door. He didn't move when the door clanked open, nor when Bob shook him by the shoulder.

Douglas sniffed. There was a strange odour in the air near Van Polk, like bitter almonds. He rushed forward and roughly turned Van Polk face upwards. Then he saw something he'd read about but never seen: the rictus of fatal cyanide poisoning, where the facial muscles go into spasm, drawing and twisting the features into a ghastly parody of a laugh.

Chapter Twenty-six

That evening a chastened but contented Doug went to visit Jean Montrose. Exhausted, he flopped down in the big green easy-chair in the living room that he used when Steven wasn't sitting in it.

'My goodness,' he said, 'what a day! Thank God it's over.'

Jean, together with the rest of her family, had watched the highlights of the drama unfold on the local evening news. They had seen a flashback to the night before, with Jamieson arresting the wanted South African murderer Roger Van Polk as he tried to escape, then a shot of them taking Van Polk, handcuffed, from a police van into the headquarters building. Then followed the first news conference, when a distraught-looking Doug Niven told the press that the killer of Moira Glashan Dalgleish had committed suicide in his police cell.

Moira Dalgleish was mentioned only in passing, and the other Dalgleish family members not at all.

The news item was followed by a commentary on the problem of overcrowding in Scottish jails, together with statistics on the increasing number of suicides of persons in custody.

Fiona came in and sat quietly in the chair next to Doug. Usually when he showed up after the end of a dramatic case she would be all over him, but today she seemed content merely to sit next to him.

'They're having a board of enquiry, of course,' said Douglas, sprawling back in the chair, 'but Bob McLeod says it'll be a quickie.' He grinned. 'He was already writing up the recommendations when I left.'

'You mean it's going to be a whitewash?' asked Fiona.

Douglas's mouth opened slightly and he looked at Fiona with astonishment.

'Between you and me?' he asked, and Fiona nodded.

'Yes. It'll be a whitewash, and so it should be.'

Now it was Fiona's turn to look surprised.

'You see, Fiona,' said Douglas, 'if we set up a real investigation every time something went wrong with the system, we'd never get anything accomplished. Everybody would be too scared of getting the blame. This time we have to do it because of public opinion, but it would be far more useful if the people on the investigating board gave their time instead to overseeing prisoners in the jail.'

Fiona didn't look convinced, and Douglas realized that perhaps he hadn't presented his case as well as he might have.

'Look at what happened today,' he went on, anxious to make Fiona understand, 'that man, Van Polk, died because he had a cyanide capsule implanted under his skin, not because there wasn't enough supervision in the cells.' Douglas's voice rose. 'And the real tragedy is that here we are, talking about him, getting all concerned about Van Polk, killer of his wife, killer of Moira Glashan. What about his victims, what about Moira? Doesn't anybody care about what happened to her? And her baby, and the rest of her family?' Douglas was breathing hard; he had inadvertently mounted his hobby-horse, which was the insidious and progressive manacling of the forces of law and order, and the simultaneous encouragement and coddling of criminals by elaborate laws that made a mockery of the efforts of the police and other law-enforcement workers.

Doug stood up, feeling a certain lack of sympathy emanating from Fiona and even from Jean.

Jean looked up from the NHS forms on her knees.

'Douglas,' she said, 'you do know it wasn't Van Polk who killed Moira, don't you?'

He stopped in his tracks, then turned slowly, his face a picture of consternation. His mouth opened, but nothing came out.

'I don't know if you'll ever be able to get a conviction, but that's your business. The evidence is all circumstantial, I'm afraid.'

'Rory, huh?' said Douglas, recouping fast. 'I knew—'

'I really don't like to do this, Doug,' said Jean, hardly aware that she had interrupted him. 'But we're dealing with a very evil person here . . .'

Jean was obviously trying to decide on a course of action, and didn't like any of the alternatives.

'There's only one way that'll work,' she said finally. 'I'll get that person to come to the surgery tomorrow afternoon. But I'll have to be sure you're there, because there's going to be some considerable risk involved.'

'I don't like the sound of this,' said Douglas. He was staring at Jean, his mind working overtime. 'Why can't you just tell me who it is, and why you think he . . .'

'Or she,' put in Jean. 'Because if I did that, the person would get off scot free,' she said tartly. 'Using police methods, you wouldn't have a chance, because we're dealing with a very intelligent person. If we do it my way, there's a chance. Not much of one, but a chance.'

'All right, then,' said Douglas, mystified. He had gone over the whole list of alternative suspects in his mind and come up blank. He had been so sure it was Armand . . . 'What do you want me to do?'

'Come to my surgery tomorrow afternoon,' said Jean. 'Can you make it at a quarter to five? Exactly?'

'I suppose so.'

'And bring that little address book of Moira's, would you?'

'Are you sure you can't tell me who this person is?' asked Douglas, concerned. 'I hate to think I'm letting you get into a dangerous situation.'

'It'll be a surprise,' said Jean, smiling. She asked him to bring some other materials with him, then added, 'Don't forget the address book.'

Next morning, when Jean arrived at the surgery, she asked Eleanor for the list of patients coming in that afternoon. She scanned the list: Rory McDermott was coming to get his stitches out; Bella had fixed an appointment because her neck was still hurting and she couldn't talk properly; and near the bottom of the list was Emily McNab's name. 'What's her problem?' asked Jean, although she had a pretty good idea.

'She didn't say,' replied Eleanor, suppressing an irritated shrug. It always annoyed her when patients wouldn't disclose their problems to her.

'Well,' said Jean, looking at their names again, 'that sounds like quite a family gathering, doesn't it?'

'Yes, Dr Montrose.' Eleanor's servile attitude was beginning to get on Jean's nerves; she definitely preferred her previous surliness and lack of respect.

'Oh, by the way,' said Jean casually, still looking at the list, 'did Lady Elspeth phone?'

'Yes, she did.' Eleanor sounded surprised. 'She said you wanted to see her. She fetched the baby from Edinburgh and she's bringing him.'

After lunch, Jean went into Helen's office to explain what she was proposing to do. Helen was not at all enthused, but agreed to see patients, take phone calls and generally handle everything else while Jean was otherwise occupied in her office.

Helen went over to the reception area and told Eleanor. 'And don't you accidentally barge into Dr

Montrose's office while she has anyone in there, do you understand?' she said in her sergeant-major voice, pointing a finger at Eleanor. 'If you have anything to tell Dr Montrose, you tell it to me instead.'

At ten minutes to five, the outside door opened, and Elspeth Dalgleish walked in, looking nervous and unsure of herself, as usual, and carrying the sleeping baby Denys all bundled up in a plastic crib.

'Oh good,' said Jean, tickling Denys gently under his chin, 'Isn't he beautiful? Elspeth, thank you for being on time, and I promise you we'll take good care of Denys. Can you come back in forty-five minutes or so?'

'Certainly,' replied Elspeth. 'I'll go and do some shopping. There's a bottle of milk in the crib if he needs it.'

Jean took the baby, who was still sleeping, into her office and placed the crib on the desk. Doug was sitting in the patient's chair, his briefcase at his feet, reading a medical magazine. 'I think I'm getting a cold,' he said, and sneezed to prove it.

Jean looked at the clock. 'All right, you'd better go into the lab now, Douglas. You'll find a chair and a table in there, and if you need to cough or sneeze, you can go out into the reception area through the other door.'

Doug went into the little lab, opened his briefcase and took out a pair of earphones and a small tape recorder. He had already placed a tiny microphone under Jean's desk. Jean closed the door and sat down to wait, butterflies dancing a highland fling in her stomach.

Chapter Twenty-seven

At five o'clock exactly, Jean heard the sound of somebody coming into the surgery, then the murmur of voices. There was a knock on the door, and Eleanor came in. 'Mr Dalgleish is here to see you,' she said.

'Please send him in,' replied Jean.

Alastair came in looking dapper and cheerful. 'Well, here I am,' he said. 'And what can I—' He stopped abruptly when he saw the crib, and came forward to look inside. 'Isn't that Denys?' he asked. 'What's he doing here?' His voice suddenly brusque.

'Do sit down,' said Jean, her throat dry. 'I'll explain as we go along.'

'Dr Montrose,' said Alastair, his eyes going from the crib to Jean, 'I only have a few moments. I have a dinner engagement in Edinburgh this evening.'

'I'll try to be as quick as I can,' said Jean apologetically. She could feel her heart racing in her chest. 'You see, Alastair, I've been thinking a lot about you in the last few days.'

Alastair looked surprised, and his alert, suspicious look softened marginally. He sat down, his glance flicking again fron Jean to the crib.

'You and your family have had a very difficult time over the last few years,' said Jean, putting her hands in her lap and pushing her chair back from the desk.

'Everybody knows that. And most people feel very sympathetic.'

Alastair's eyebrows started to come together, and Jean went on. 'First there's your older brother, Sir Farquar Dalgleish. It must have been terrible when he died. About four years ago, wasn't it? I heard that the two of you had been out shooting grouse—'

'Dr Montrose,' Alastair interrupted, 'did you ask me to come here to tell me about my family's history?'

'No, of course not,' said Jean, flustered. 'I just don't want to leave out anything that's important. Anyway the inquest found it to be an accidental death. But you know how people talk. And when Colin took over the title and the estates, I imagine you thought he'd be easier to, well . . . *manipulate* is such a strong word . . .'

Alastair flushed angrily and moved on his chair but he didn't say anything.

There was a knock at the door and Helen poked her head in. 'Excuse me,' she said to Jean, 'I just want you to know that Eleanor's gone and I'm leaving. There are a couple of messages I've left for you on the desk.' She smiled at both of them. 'Goodnight.'

When the door closed, Jean went on. 'Sir Ian's death occurred soon after you left the Department of Immigration with your two colleagues, didn't it?' Jean checked the chronology on a sheet of paper in front of her. Her voice was sympathetic. 'That must have been a terrible time for you, but the three of you all did so well. One became Scottish Secretary, the other a Cabinet Minister and here you are: an up-and-coming MP on the verge of becoming a major political figure.' Jean paused, the admiration clear in her voice.

Alastair's expression softened marginally. 'Yes,' he said in his deep orator's voice, 'these have been very difficult times for all of us.'

'And, of course, a big scandal at this stage,' said Jean, her voice changing, 'one you couldn't cover up, would have been fatal to your political career, wouldn't it?'

Alastair froze in his chair.

'And, of course, you needed money,' went on Jean, thinking how tight her throat felt and how much she'd like a cup of tea, but she didn't dare stop. 'It must be a terrible drain on one's financial resources, being a top politician . . . And doubly infuriating, when there is all that potential cash in the Dalgleish estates, all that undeveloped land . . .' Jean sighed in sympathy with Alastair. 'Poor Colin . . . well, he wouldn't consider selling any land, or so Elspeth told me. It was a dilemma for you, a real dilemma, because if Colin got shot or died in some other way, people would be bound to remember Sir Ian and start asking questions.'

Alastair sat back, looking at Jean as if she had horns coming out of her head, but he still didn't say anything. Jean figured he'd wait until he found out exactly how much she knew. The knowledge that Douglas was within fifteen feet of her gave a little courage, but Alastair was even closer.

She glanced at the baby, who was still blissfully asleep, then pushed a computer print-out along the desk towards Alastair. It was headed: *Patient's name: Colin Dalgleish. Specimen: Blood sample. Physician: Dr Jean Montrose.* It contained a row of symbols and numbers:

Na.	145 mEq/L
Pb.	less than 1ppm
Hg.	182 ppm
As.	less than 1 ppm
Cu.	less than 5 ppm
Au.	less than 1 ppm

Other heavy metals: insignificant amounts detected.

'I felt pretty sure that Sir Colin was being poisoned,' went on Jean when Alastair had read through the list, 'and he certainly had the classical signs of mercury poisoning.' Jean pointed at the middle of the print-out. 'I'm sure you know that Hg means mercury, short for the Latin name Hydrargyrum. It was a good choice; and putting it in a vitamin preparation he took every day was a clever idea. Mercury doesn't show up in the ordinary lab tests, and the mental deterioration that occurs would allow you eventually to take legal custody of the estates, by that time to everybody's relief. Then, as my father used to say, you'd be happy as a pig in clover.'

Alastair's eyebrows went up and he flushed.

'Oh dear,' said Jean, 'that wasn't very nice, was it? I'm sorry.'

At least the print-out stimulated a reaction. 'This is sheer nonsense,' said Alastair, pushing the sheet back across the desk, 'Whatever you've come up with has no links to me. Even if your story is true, any one of half-a-dozen people could have been responsible.'

Jean sighed, acknowledging such a possibility, but not letting it stop the flow of her thoughts. 'And then, when things are going quite nicely with your long-term plan, along comes Moira . . .'

Jean waited for some sort of response, but all Alastair did was start tapping on his knee: tap, tap, tap. There was something disconcerting about it, maybe because he made no sound.

'I suppose it was understandable about Moira,' Jean continued. 'She'd always been your favourite, and then she became a woman . . . a woman who prided herself on her seductiveness. She would have been hard to resist, and she'd have a good opportunity to work on you when you went hiking together.'

Jean paused for a moment. In spite of everything, she felt sorry for Alastair; he really hadn't anticipated Moira.

Alastair's colour had changed almost imperceptibly, and he glanced quickly around the room, noting the position of the doors.

'And then Moira became pregnant. I'm sure you were generous, gave her enough money to go to Hong Kong or wherever.' Jean shook her head. 'It must have cost you a great deal to keep her from exposing you as the father there and then.'

There was a tiny sound from the direction of the adjoining room, and Alastair bounded out of his chair and flung open the door. The lab was empty. Alastair closed the door, walked over to the other one and locked it. When he sat down again, his expression was frightening. 'Go on,' he said; it was clearly an order.

'Moira's choice of her imaginary-husband's name showed she wasn't too happy with you,' said Jean. 'After all, Glashan Dalgleish was one of your less-reputable ancestors, one-eyed and scarred by smallpox, if I remember . . .'

Alastair's lips tightened. Obviously, he hadn't been delighted by her choice either.

'And he, too, had ravished his brother's daughter,' went on Jean. 'Interesting, how history has a way of repeating itself.'

There was a brief pause while Jean caught up the thread of her thoughts. 'Do you remember, Alastair, when we were looking at the photograph that Moira had on her bedside table, you told me you met her husband and had dinner with him at your club in London? Well, as you very well know, that photograph was a publicity shot of an unknown actor.'

'Dr Montrose,' said Alastair, 'you have woven an entire tissue of lies from a very flimsy premise. I would remind you of the laws of libel—'

'If anything, Alastair, it would be *slander*,' said Jean mildly. 'However, I'm just talking to you, and, anyway, it's all true, as you know. You see, I knew about you and the baby the first time I saw him, but I saw no need to disclose the fact that incest had occurred.'

'Most kind of you, I'm sure, doctor,' said Alastair, in a bored tone. 'And how did you come to the conclusion I was his father?'

'Easy,' said Jean, her voice taking on a new crispness.

'The baby has his fourth and fifth toes joined together. It's a genetic trait that all you Dalgleish men have. But that particular trait is transmitted only through the Y-chromosome. In other words, the trait comes down only through the males. Which means that it was a male member of the Dalgleish family who fathered young Denys Dalgleish Glashan here. I considered Sir Colin, briefly,' Jean went on, 'but as you probably know, chronic mercury poisoning not only makes the victims nervous, tearful and schizoid, but also impotent.'

A thin line of sweat appeared on Alastair's hairline but he remained silent.

Jean glanced at the clock. 'Oh dear,' she said. 'I didn't think this would take so long . . . Anyway, to come back to Moira, somehow she'd found out about Armand Thierry; either because you told her or, more likely, because she went through your files. I noticed the new locks on your filing cabinets. She started to blackmail Armand Thierry, then you, too, after the baby was conceived. That's how she was able to get a car and all those expensive clothes.'

Alastair smiled. 'Moira had a lot of boyfriends. I'm sure they gave her money for those expenses.'

Jean shook her head decisively. 'No. I don't think so. Moira certainly didn't pick them for their thick wallets. Look at Rory McDermott, or that schoolteacher before him. No,' she went on, 'you eventually balked . . .' Jean opened the little address book at the list under the initial A and showed it to him. 'She recorded every one of your payments. The last one was particularly small. I suppose that's why she decided to go public and tell the whole story to Arnie Larkin at the *Courier*, and that's when you decided you had to kill her.'

Alastair looked at the locked door for a second. 'I know about the Hippocratic Oath,' he said quietly. 'It means you can't divulge anything that's said in confidence to you. You're a very clever woman, but there are a lot of things you can't possibly understand. I hated myself for killing her; I was really very fond of her, but sooner or later she was going to tell everybody about our baby,' Alastair glanced at the crib with a strange, tender expression, 'and I just couldn't allow that, for obvious reasons. Anyway, the case is closed. Van Polk is dead, and as far as everybody is concerned, he was the killer.' Alastair paused. 'That is, everybody but you.'

'I think you'd better go now,' said Jean. It was the pre-arranged signal for Douglas to march in from the next room.

Nothing happened.

Suddenly, without seeming to have moved, Alastair was behind her, bending forward, talking softly and insistently. 'I'm taking the risk of being detained at her Majesty's pleasure,' he said, very quietly, his mouth close to Jean's ear, 'but as you know I have friends in high places. And as you're the only one who knows what happened . . .This won't take very long, Dr Montrose, I promise you.'

His fingers slipped very gently around her neck, and Jean, petrified by Doug's non-appearance, tried to scream but she couldn't because her windpipe was already narrowed. In a sudden, almost convulsive movement, Jean reached up and caught Alastair's thick dark hair with both hands, yanked him forward so that his midriff slammed against the back of her chair, then with all the strength she possessed, smashed his head down on the corner of her desk. Alastair slithered to the floor, and at the same moment, Douglas irrupted into the room, sneezing as he entered.

'Oh my God, I'm so sorry, Jean,' he said, appalled by what he saw. 'I was sneezing and had to keep leaving the lab . . .'

Jean, feeling weak, scared, and very angry, put her hand on her chest. Her heart was pounding so fast she couldn't count the beat.

'Douglas Niven,' she said breathlessly, 'this is

positively the very last time I'm getting involved in one of your cases.' She bent down to check Alastair's pulse. 'He's just concussed. Now, please, get both him and you out of here. Elspeth should be back any minute now to pick up the baby.'

A selection of bestsellers from Headline

THE CAT WHO WASN'T THERE	Lilian Jackson Braun	£4.50 ☐
THE SNARES OF DEATH	Kate Charles	£4.99 ☐
THE POISONED CHALICE	Michael Clynes	£4.50 ☐
MURDER WEARS A COWL	P C Doherty	£4.50 ☐
COLD IN THE EARTH	Anne Granger	£4.99 ☐
MURDER MOST HOLY	Paul Harding	£4.50 ☐
RECIPE FOR DEATH	Janet Laurence	£4.50 ☐
MURDER UNDER THE KISSING BOUGH	Amy Myers	£4.99 ☐
A FATAL END	Ann Quinton	£4.99 ☐
FATAL FEVER	C F Roe	£4.50 ☐
DYING CHEEK TO CHEEK	Diane K Shah	£4.99 ☐

All Headline books are available at your local bookshop or newsagent, or can be ordered direct from the publisher. Just tick the titles you want and fill in the form below. Prices and availability subject to change without notice.

Headline Book Publishing PLC, Cash Sales Department, Bookpoint, 39 Milton Park, Abingdon, OXON, OX14 4TD, UK. If you have a credit card you may order by telephone — 0235 831700.

Please enclose a cheque or postal order made payable to Bookpoint Ltd to the value of the cover price and allow the following for postage and packing:
UK & BFPO: £1.00 for the first book, 50p for the second book and 30p for each additional book ordered up to a maximum charge of £3.00.
OVERSEAS & EIRE: £2.00 for the first book, £1.00 for the second book and 50p for each additional book.

Name ....

Address ....

....

....

If you would prefer to pay by credit card, please complete:
Please debit my Visa/Access/Diner's Card/American Express (delete as applicable) card no:

Signature ....Expiry Date ....